Exhilarated

After Lily's audition was through, she wished there was someone waiting for her in the audience — Jonathan, or one of her girlfriends — anyone who could share her excitement. Oh, well, Lily thought carelessly, taking the stage stairs with an extra bounce.

Then all at once she noticed there *was* someone waiting for her, kind of. As she reached the bottom step, Lily found herself looking straight into Buford Wodjovodski's sky-blue eyes. His face broke into a smile. Lily smiled back with equal warmth. For the long moment that Buford held her gaze, they might as well have been the only two people in the theater.

COUPLES

HOLD ME TIGHT

M.E. Cooper

SCHOLASTIC INC.
New York Toronto London Auckland Sydney

ISBN 0-590-41689-8

12 11 10 9 8 7 6 5 4 3 2   9/8 0 1 2 3/9

Printed in the U.S.A.   01

First Scholastic printing, September 1988

Chapter

1

"So, Char, what are you planning to do to make our senior year one we'll never forget?" Josh Ferguson ran a hand through his dark wavy hair and grinned amiably at Charlotte DeVries as he tossed her the question.

Charlotte smiled back, her bright blue eyes sparkling vivaciously. "You want the whole calendar, Josh?" she teased in an exaggerated southern drawl. "You'll miss your first class if I tell you every single amazingly fun activity I've got up my sleeve!" Her friends laughed, and Char laughed, too. It was so easy to be in a good mood on a morning like this, she thought, taking a deep breath of crisp autumn air. It was only the second week of school, and she still had that tingly beginning-of-the-school-year feeling. Maybe everything felt especially fresh for her because this would be Charlotte's first full year at Kennedy High; last winter her family had moved to

1

Rose Hill, Maryland, from Alabama, where Char was born. At first she wasn't sure she'd like it "up north," but she'd made friends in no time at all. In fact, she'd gotten so involved so fast at Kennedy that she was elected to the student government as student activities director. It was a position of real responsibility, and Charlotte was very aware that she had big shoes to fill. Jonathan Preston, a recent Kennedy graduate and last year's activities director, had been almost maniacally enthusiastic. He'd hardly have time to catch his breath after one blockbuster event when he'd plunge into plans for another.

But Char wasn't too worried about being a flop at the job. Ever since she was six years old, hostessing "tea parties" for all her friends in Alabama, she'd loved arranging and organizing social events. And it really wasn't *that* big a step from a kiddy tea party to a high school dance! she thought to herself mischievously. Besides, Kennedy students were famous for their willingness to pitch in and help, especially the crowd of kids she was hanging around with these days. She guessed she'd never have to look for volunteers when she needed them.

Charlotte studied her companions' faces without appearing to do so. Everyone was decked out in new fall sweaters and scarves. Lounging on the benches they traditionally staked out as their special spot — a patch of the main quad between two trees — they looked like a page from a clothing catalogue. They were all talking and laughing, enjoying the last few minutes before the first bell rang.

2

Josh had his arm around his girlfriend, Frankie Baker, who peeked earnestly through her pale blonde bangs as she turned to say something to Lily Rorshack. Lily laughed and turned to repeat it to Stacy Morrison, whose boyfriend, Zachary McGraw, was teasing her by wrapping his new plaid scarf around her face and mouth, mummy-style. Meanwhile, Greg Montgomery and Daniel Tackett, the new student body president and school newspaper editor-in-chief respectively, had fallen into a heated discussion about some political issue. Then there was Vince DiMase. . . .

Charlotte felt her cheeks flush as she looked into Vince's dark, serious eyes. He half-smiled at her, and she turned away quickly, unintentionally darting a guilty glance at her best friend, Roxanne Easton, who was sitting next to her on the far end of one of the benches. Fortunately Rox, who was unusually quiet that morning, hadn't seemed to notice Char's eye contact with Vince. Relieved, Charlotte relaxed even as she concentrated doubly hard on not looking anywhere near Vince. She stifled a small, sad sigh. There was only one cloud hanging over Char these days, and that was the fact that she'd fallen for a guy who just happened to be her best friend's ex. Vince might be Mr. Right for any other girl, but because of her concern for Roxanne's feelings, Vince was Mr. Wrong for Charlotte.

Char was distracted from this gloomy consideration by a hand waving in front of her face. "Hey, Scarlett O'Hara!" Lily was saying. "You never answered Josh's question! There might not

3

be enough time to give us the entire activities agenda, but what's the first item?"

Char snapped back to reality. "Why, the Welcome Dance, of course," she announced with a toss of her sunny blonde hair. "Don't tell me it's not already the talk of the town!"

"It is," Frankie assured Charlotte. "Lily's just got her head in the Drama Club clouds as usual! I, for one, can't wait for the Welcome Dance. Don't they have one every year at Kennedy?"

Charlotte remembered that Frankie and most of the others — Roxanne, Zack, Stacy, Lily, and Daniel included — were also new to the JFK scene, having also transferred to Kennedy the previous winter when nearby Stevenson High School was closed down. "A fall dance *is* traditional," she explained to Frankie, "but this one is going to be something special, I promise you. Wait till you hear what I have in mind!" She crossed her ankles and leaned forward with her hands clasped on her knees. "I decided streamers and balloons and a band were all well and good but weren't quite enough for my debut as student activities director. I really want to make a splash! So . . ." Charlotte paused theatrically, enjoying the fact that everyone's eyes were on her. She wasn't the type of person who had to be the center of attention to be happy, but she certainly didn't mind a captive audience now and then. "So," she continued brightly, "I talked to Principal Beman" — she rolled her eyes with mock self-importance — "and he's given me permission to hold the dance in the Little Theater instead of in the gym."

Charlotte waited for a reaction. As she ex-

4

pected, the crowd exchanged questioning glances. "How come?" Zachary finally asked, puzzled.

Char dimpled slyly. "Well, you know the big screen in the Little Theater, where they show movies sometimes?" Zack nodded. "How would you like to see your own handsome face flashed up there, a hundred times larger than life, during the dance?"

Zack's blue eyes popped wide open in surprise. Char giggled. "Don't worry, not just your face — yours and the entire football team's. We're going to show video clips from the first few games at the dance!"

Char smiled her triumph as the crowd hooted with approval. "What a great idea!" Greg exclaimed in his deep, commanding voice.

"I thought so, too," Charlotte admitted. She didn't bother to hide her happy satisfaction. "Kennedy won the first big game, thanks to Zack here, and by the time the dance rolls around, we're sure to have a few more stirring victories under our belts. I think scenes from the games and shots of the crowds will provide just the right festive fall atmosphere."

"I couldn't agree more!" declared Stacy proudly, leaning over to plant a kiss on her boyfriend's cheek.

Zachary flushed with shy pleasure. The first game against Carrolton Day School the previous Friday *had* been a strong win, and Char knew Zack felt especially good about playing well because it was his first time on the field for his new team. He didn't think of himself as a star, but it was already clear to the whole student body

5

that with Zachary as quarterback, the Kennedy squad was heading for a dynamite season.

Lily, her forehead wrinkled, was the only person who didn't appear unreservedly enthusiastic about Charlotte's proposition. "But, Char, maybe this is a stupid question, but how can you hold a *dance* in a *theater*?" she asked. "I mean, with all the seats and everything? Correct me if I'm wrong, but I have spent a lot of time in the Little Theater, and I really think it would get kind of cramped if the whole school tried to dance in the aisles!"

"Exactly," acknowledged Charlotte with a small frown. She toyed with the ruffled cuffs of her lacy white blouse. "That's the big catch here, and that's where I'm going to need help from all of you. Mr. Beman okayed holding the dance in the theater on the condition that I arrange to have the chairs moved myself. I guess the custodial and grounds staff will all be busy that Friday getting ready for the game. So I said I'd round up some students to do the work during lunch."

"I'd be happy to help," Greg volunteered promptly.

"Me, too," Zack offered. "But only if you can promise me I won't pull any muscles." He flexed his arm, grinning. "Got to save my strength for the game that night."

"Thanks, you guys," said Charlotte with an appreciative smile.

"I'd love to move chairs, Char, but I have a spirit rally that lunch period," said Stacy, who was a cheerleader as well as one of Kennedy's top gymnasts.

"Hey, I'm free!" Josh announced after a moment's consideration. "I almost forgot I'd decided to let my new assistant man WKND on Fridays from now on." Josh managed the school radio station, which broadcast a special news and music program every day during lunch. "You can count on me."

Avoiding Vince, Charlotte directed her gaze expectantly at the only other boy who hadn't spoken up. Daniel raised his hands sheepishly. "Char, I really wish I could join you, but I just can't spare a minute away from the newspaper. I've got the staff in the office every single day during lunch period and after school, too, and I can't ask them to work like that unless I'm there working right next to them. Sorry."

Char nodded. "I understand, Daniel," she said sincerely. "You're new to your job just like I am to mine. I think we feel the same way about working hard and doing well."

Daniel briskly adjusted his dark Wayfarer sunglasses. "You got it. I'm going to do more than that, though," he assured her and the others, his voice growing animated. "*The Red and the Gold* is going to be better this year than anything this school has ever seen!" Daniel's ambition was a personal trademark, and Charlotte knew it had almost gotten him into real trouble when he'd first transferred from Stevenson, where he'd been editor of the *Stevenson Sentinel*. There was a lot of tension at first between the new Stevenson students and the old Kennedy crowd, and Daniel had been one of the most discontented transfers. Convinced that he was being treated unfairly by

7

the Kennedy "establishment," he had pulled a fast one on Karen Davis, the former editor-in-chief of *The Red and the Gold*, by setting her up to write a fake interview. Not only was the article printed, but it was also submitted to an important high school journalism contest. The prank had gotten completely out of hand. Fortunately, Frankie and Josh were able to sneak the article out of contest headquarters.

It was a long time before Daniel was able to redeem himself in Karen's eyes. They had ended up respecting one another, however, and it was a tribute to Daniel's considerable journalistic talents that Karen had selected him to be her replacement despite the fact that he'd only been at Kennedy for one semester.

"I don't know that much about putting together a newspaper," Lily was confessing to Daniel. "What's your tactic for breaking new ground?"

"It's all in the staff," he informed her matter-of-factly. "New people, new ideas — I've even created two new positions." Daniel always talked with his hands and now his gestures communicated his enthusiasm. "Do you guys know Sara Gates and Jana Lacey? They're both juniors. Sara is really bright — I have very high hopes for her. She's *The Red and the Gold*'s first movie reviewer. And Jana's going to write about travel. Hot, huh?"

The crowd was in general agreement. "Jana Lacey, eh?" Greg's sea-green eyes glinted with interest. "She's Peter Lacey's younger sister, right? Well, if she's anything like him, you'll be lucky to have her on your team. Peter's a great guy."

Peter Lacey had been a "big man on campus" a few years before and he was one of Josh's predecessors at WKND. Peter's influence was still felt at the radio station, where his collection of Bruce Springsteen albums continued to reign supreme on the airwaves.

"I don't know anything about Peter," Stacy interrupted. "But Jana . . ." Stacy wrinkled her upturned nose in distaste. "I have French with her again this semester, and every day she spends the whole period passing on the latest Kennedy scandal to anyone within whispering distance. No offense, Daniel, but she might have been better suited to a gossip column than travel articles. She even spreads rumors in foreign languages!"

Charlotte couldn't help laughing, but she tried to be fair to Jana. "Yeah, but, Stace, everyone indulges in a little gossip now and then," she reminded her friend.

Stacy shook her head. "Not like Jana, Char. With her it's an art form. We're talking *vicious*. I'd watch out if I were you, Daniel!"

Daniel waved away Stacy's warning. "*The Red and the Gold* is a newspaper, not a kaffee klatsch," he said in a disinterested tone. "I'm more concerned about my staff's professional abilities than their personal quirks. Jana's a good writer, and she's well-traveled. It's as simple as that."

Stacy smiled good-naturedly. "You win, Mr. Tackett. As usual." Just then the bell rang. Reluctantly, the gang gathered up their books and jackets, said their good-byes, and headed for their respective homerooms.

Charlotte and Roxanne had homeroom and

9

then first period English together, but Char waved Rox on as she sat back down on the bench to retie one of her shoes. "I'll catch up with you!" Charlotte called to her friend. Roxanne nodded and turned toward the school building. When Charlotte looked up a moment later after retying her laces, she was surprised to see that she wasn't alone on the quad. Vince had remained behind, too. For the second time that morning, Charlotte felt herself blush hotly.

Vince sat down next to her, carefully keeping a couple of feet of bench between them. "Uh, Charlotte," he began gruffly. "I just wanted to let you know that I'd be happy to help you out with the Little Theater job if you want me to. I didn't say anything before, though, because — well, I knew it might not be the best move, with Rox there and everything. But I wanted you to know you can count on me."

Charlotte gazed into Vince's dark brown eyes and then forced herself to look away before she could get lost in them. Why did he have to be so darn thoughtful and considerate? she asked herself silently. Just when she was trying her hardest to ignore her feelings for him, he made her like him even more!

It didn't help that Char knew Vince cared for her as much as she cared for him. They'd gotten to know each other that summer at a week-long leadership camp for D.C.-area high school seniors. Four kids had represented Kennedy at the conference — Char, Vince, Daniel, and Roxanne. It was at leadership camp that Charlotte had gotten close to Rox Easton as well. Her new friend had immediately confided in Charlotte about how torn apart she was over her breakup with Vince. Char was still relatively vague on exactly what had happened to cause Vince to call things off, but she hadn't wanted to pry into what remained an extremely painful subject for Roxanne. Now Charlotte recalled those intimate conversations with a pang. She'd given Rox all the support and advice possible, and a close bond had formed between them. Char knew Roxanne would have done the same for her; she now considered Rox her best friend in Rose Hill. But at the same time, from her talks with Vince at the leadership conference and afterward, she understood more and more why Roxanne had been crushed when he had cut short their relationship. Vince was sweet, handsome, kind, fun. . . .

But there was no point in thinking about all this. Charlotte's loyalty to Roxanne made her determined not to give in to her growing attraction to Vince. She hadn't been entirely successful. . . . Charlotte blushed yet again as she recalled their encounter at the recent Maryland State Fair. She had wandered away from her friends and bumped into Vince by one of the concession stands. Relatively alone in the bustle of the crowd, they'd shared a secret, passionate kiss. Fortunately, no one they knew saw them, and Char had sworn to herself and to Vince that she wouldn't ever let it happen again. He was Roxanne's ex. Even worse, Rox still liked him. Char would never hurt her best friend, no matter how much she might be attracted to Vince herself.

Vince had kept his distance since the fair. Even

though he felt his relationship with Roxanne was definitely over, he respected Charlotte's feelings for her friend and her reluctance to go out with him. Still, it was hard to keep up a façade of indifference in front of everyone. Char felt the strain, and she could tell by the moody, glum expression on Vince's face that he felt it, too.

She took a deep breath. It was so stupid not to allow Vince to help move chairs. But it would be wrong. She had to avoid any and all contact with him or her friendship with Rox would be over. Char pushed the hair back from her forehead and grabbed her books, practically jumping to her feet. "Thanks — thanks for the offer, Vince," she said, the sad look in her eyes belying the cheerful note in her voice. "But, well, I just don't think your helping me with the chairs would be a good idea."

Vince shrugged, his broad shoulders sagging somewhat. "I understand." He looked disappointed, but he spoke sincerely. Charlotte smiled, grateful.

Vince seemed to take her smile as encouragement. He cleared his throat, preparing to speak again. "Char — "

Charlotte cut him off. She couldn't let him corner her into having a serious — and therefore dangerous — conversation. "I really have to run." Flashing him her brightest smile, she added, "Don't you be late for class, either, Vince! 'Bye now."

Turning away, Charlotte hurried off. As she went, she felt Vince's eyes on her back. For a

12

moment she couldn't help wishing, as much as she liked Roxanne, that being a true best friend wasn't so hard.

Roxanne stood on the cement walkway that led into the south wing, watching Charlotte and Vince through a lock of tawny, windblown hair. The sight made Roxanne feel sick inside, sick and furious. Even from that distance the spark between the two was clearly visible. Rox tried to think back to leadership camp to recall if it had been present even then. She drew a blank. She'd been too preoccupied at the time with winning Vince back. Roxanne was filled with shame at the memory of Vince's flat-out rejection of her. It was true that at first she'd just been using him, hoping that by dating a boy who was part of the "in" crowd she could finally become a part of it herself. Every other effort she'd made in that direction since she'd transferred the previous winter had failed miserably. But to Roxanne's surprise, she'd actually ended up falling heavily for warm, chivalrous Vince and his loving family, which was so very different from her own. Vince was the first guy she'd met at Kennedy who treated her like a real person. Rox wouldn't have admitted to herself that that was probably because he didn't really know her. All she cared about was that she had almost succeeded in wrapping Vince around her little finger — permanently. Then stupid Frankie Baker had blown everything! She'd finally gotten up the nerve to blast Roxanne for using Vince — and when she did, Vince happened to walk up and hear *everything*! Roxanne pursed her glossed lips angrily. She would never forgive Frankie for that. Never.

Ever since that awful moment, Vince had been deaf to Roxanne's many attempts to explain herself and to assure him she really cared for him. And ever since the state fair when Rox had witnessed Vince and Char in their passionate embrace, it was only too clear why. Vince was all ears only for the sweet-as-honey words of that sly southern belle Charlotte, whom Rox had naively considered her best friend!

Roxanne swallowed her anger as Charlotte, now leaving Vince behind to dash across the quad, flagged her down. Char joined her, breathless, and they headed into the building together.

"Are your shoes all tied up?" Roxanne inquired as she slipped out of her brown leather jacket.

Charlotte didn't pick up on Rox's thinly veiled sarcasm. "Yes. Now I won't be tripping all the way to homeroom!" she declared cheerfully. Then her smile dissolved into a look of concern. "Rox, is anything the matter?" Char asked. "You were kind of quiet out on the quad just now."

"Why, what could possibly be the matter?" Rox challenged with a brittle smile. "I'm just fine."

Charlotte raised her fair eyebrows. "You're sure?"

"Absolutely!" Roxanne managed another bright white smile for Char's benefit, but inside she was steaming. When Charlotte gave her arm a friendly squeeze, it was all Rox could do not to yank it away in disgust. But she didn't want Char to know she'd discovered her treachery, at least not yet. Char could enjoy Vince and her undeserved position of prominence in the Kennedy social scene — a position that should rightfully have been Roxanne's — for a while longer.

Rox darted an if-looks-could-kill glance at Char as they took adjacent seats in their homeroom. Her new best friend had turned out to be a two-timing back-stabber, but Charlotte would be sorry she'd messed with Roxanne Easton. It was only a matter of time before Rox figured out a way to pay her back. She'd make Charlotte wish she'd never moved to Rose Hill if it was the last thing she did.

Chapter 2

Lily leaned back against her locker and crossed her arms, hugging a copy of the script of *Twelfth Night* against her chest. She peered out into the jostling crowd of Kennedy students as they hoisted their backpacks and bookbags and hustled toward the main entrance and the line of waiting school buses. Stacy and Frankie, who had offered to escort Lily to the Little Theater, where she'd be auditioning for the fall play in half an hour, were nowhere in sight. Lily bit her lip nervously. She didn't absolutely need their moral support, but it sure wouldn't hurt. She hoped her friends hadn't forgotten the plans they'd made earlier in the day at lunch.

Even though she'd auditioned for dozens of plays and had some experience with Shakespeare, Lily couldn't stop the usual audition-day butterflies in her stomach. Humming tunelessly, she tried to distract herself from her jitters by thinking back to the last play she'd been in, the musical *The Fantasticks*, the previous spring. It had been her first production at Kennedy High, and it would always hold a special place in her memory for that reason. But mostly the experience was unforgettable because it was during rehearsals for *The Fantasticks* that she'd met Jonathan Preston.

The recollection brought a bittersweet smile to Lily's delicate face. She and Jonathan had pretty much fallen in love at first sight, but like a Shakespearean romantic comedy, they'd had to go through what seemed at the time like endless confusions and misunderstandings before things worked out for them. When Jonathan met Lily, he didn't know that she was the girl his friends all held responsible for their vicious feud with the new kids from Stevenson. Lily herself had been blissfully ignorant of her supposed role in the feud. At Daniel's urging, she'd posed as a reformed street kid and jailbird for an interview with the editor of the Kennedy newspaper. Lily had been talked into believing that the Kennedy kids were blackballing them out of positions of authority. Lily and Daniel's "prank" would show them how gullible they really were. Lily hadn't learned until much later that the Kennedy students weren't terrible at all. She also discovered that Karen Davis nearly got into serious trouble by entering the interview with Lily in a journalism contest. Roxanne, Daniel, and the others from Stevenson had kept this fact from her, suspecting that she would intervene on Karen's behalf if she ever found out how far overboard their practical joke had gone.

Lily's new relationship with Jonathan was turned upside down by her presumed guilt, but things finally went right when Jonathan learned she was actually innocent of anything malicious. Lily's head still whirled when she thought of the events of the spring semester! But in the end she and Jonathan had gotten everything straight between them. And in addition to finding a new boyfriend, Lily had made some new friends, too, after discovering how shallow the loyalties of many of her old acquaintances from Stevenson had turned out to be. Lily had grown especially close to Frankie and Stacy, whom she hadn't known very well while they were all at Stevenson, over the course of the past few months. Although she was truly excited for him, a small part of Lily wished that Jonathan hadn't graduated so that he could be with her at a moment like this. But on the other hand, she was happy to rely on the support of two genuinely caring friends like Stacy and Frankie. They were certainly a lot calmer and less frantic than Jonathan!

Just then Lily was jolted from her reverie by Stacy herself. The crowd had thinned, and in the now-clear hallway Stacy was executing a few cheerleading jumps. "Give me an L, give me an I, give me an L, give me a Y. What does it spell? LILY! Go, fight, win that leading role!" Stacy shouted, her sun-streaked ponytail bouncing wildly.

Frankie joined Lily by the lockers, laughing so hard she could barely speak. "Do you know that person?" she asked Lily weakly.

Lily giggled and shook her head, her dark

blonde hair swinging across her face. "Not me!"

Stacy stuck out her tongue as she abandoned her cheer. Then she put an arm around the shoulders of her two friends and started steering them down the hall in the direction of the Little Theater. "Come on, Lil, admit it," Stacy said with a mischievous smile. "I've inspired you to try out like you've never tried out before."

"Yeah, for the football team!" Lily joked.

Stacy tossed her head in a pretend huff. "You drama types just don't recognize the *art* in everyday pursuits like cheerleading. But you'll see," she predicted. "You'll have a great audition, and then you'll thank me!"

They rounded a corner in the hallway and entered the main lobby. The Little Theater was in a separate building, a renovated colonial chapel across the street. Lily, Frankie, and Stacy now discovered that the overcast day had given way to a cold drizzle. After counting to ten, they sprinted the distance to the theater with their books held over their heads. Ducking inside, they collapsed in a slightly damp heap on a couple of chairs in the entryway. Lily caught her breath and looked around as she brushed the drops of water from the sleeves of her black jersey dress. A few other students were lingering by the posted audition list, but most of the *Twelfth Night* hopefuls must already be gathering in the theater itself.

Lily gulped and turned to Stacy and Frankie. Stacy made a goofy face and gave Lily a thumbs-up sign.

Frankie smiled encouragingly. "Are they starting the auditions now?" she asked.

Lily glanced at her watch. "Actually, not for another ten minutes," she answered. "People are probably in there looking over the scenes they're going to read from and comparing approaches to the different characters." She grimaced. "I know everyone's going to want Viola."

"I'm not too up on my Shakespeare," Stacy admitted, leaning back in her chair and pushing her hands deep in the pockets of her jeans. "That's the female lead, right?" Lily nodded. Stacy rose halfway out of her seat, pretending to head for the theater. "Want me to run in and tell them all not to bother, the role's already taken?" she offered, her brown eyes innocently wide. "I could announce it in a cheer if you want."

Laughing, Lily grabbed the sleeve of Stacy's denim jacket and yanked her back down.

"Morrison, you are such a clown," Frankie declared. "Maybe *you* should be trying out for the play!"

Stacy considered the proposal with mock seriousness. "Not a bad idea, but I really don't know where I'd find the time for rehearsals and stuff," she said regretfully. "I guess I'll just stick to cheerleading and gymnastics. That's enough extracurricular activity for me."

"I don't know how you handle all that," Lily said, tapping the toes of her pointy black boots restlessly against the floor and trying not to look in the direction of the open door to the theater, through which more students were drifting. "It's like a double workout every day!"

Stacy shrugged. "Not every day," she confessed. "Sometimes I don't have the energy for a

20

gymnastics session after cheerleading practice. But don't tell Katie that!" Frankie and Lily nodded, promising not to reveal Stacy's transgressions to Katie Crawford, Kennedy High's former star gymnast who, sidetracked in her own career by a broken leg, had coached Stacy to a spot in the league gymnastics finals the previous spring. Katie, who still dated Greg Montgomery, was now a freshman in the coaching program at the University of Florida. She and Stacy were keeping in touch by letter. "Still, I do make it to the Fitness Center four or five times a week," Stacy added in her own defense. "And that's about four or five times more than I used to in the old days!"

"Katie made a big difference, huh?" Frankie observed, her light eyes glowing softly. Lily knew that Frankie, too, had benefited from Katie's coaching in a way. Katie had been one of the first people to encourage Frankie to be herself and to break away from the oppressive influence of Roxanne, Frankie's oldest childhood friend.

"She really did make a difference for me." Stacy's eyes sparkled with affection as she remembered. "She was a tough coach, but she was also a really good friend. I never could have made it to the finals without her. I'm really going to miss her next season."

"Things are different without last year's seniors around, aren't they?" Frankie listed the names of some of their friends who'd graduated last spring. "Katie, Brian, Karen, Eric, Jeremy, Diana . . . and, of course, Jonathan," she added, swiveling in her seat so she could pat Lily on the shoulder. "Not that I mind having moved up to being a senior myself. It's fun being in charge of the Computer Club and having a piece of the action."

"Hey, how is Jonathan anyway?" Stacy asked, also turning to face Lily. "Have you heard from him lately? Does he like the University of Pennsylvania?"

Lily rolled her eyes. "Have I *heard* from him lately?" she repeated wryly. "Stacy, he calls me almost every day! At this rate his phone bill's going to be as high as his tuition."

"I think that's romantic," Frankie said with a dreamy sigh. "He misses you so much!"

Lily wrinkled her nose. "Yeah, I guess he does. But it's not just missing me. It's his general panic about college and everything. Sometimes I feel like I've become more of a security blanket than a girlfriend. *You* know what I mean."

Frankie and Stacy nodded sympathetically. Lily's boyfriend had been a bundle of nervous energy all that past spring and summer. Superinvolved in school, he'd had a hard time coming to terms with the reality of graduation and the prospect of creating a new life after Kennedy High. In fact, Jonathan had gotten so flipped out that he'd neglected his spring term classwork and almost didn't graduate at all. It had been a stressful time in his relationship with Lily, but she had done her best to be supportive through it all. Even her closest friends didn't know how much the ongoing effort to calm Jonathan down had tired her out, though. But there was something even more unsettling on her mind. . . .

Lily suddenly began speaking without thinking first. "And then there's that promise we made."

"What promise?" Stacy and Frankie asked in unison.

Lily immediately wished she hadn't said anything. Even though Frankie and Stacy were her friends, she didn't really want anyone to know about her vow to Jonathan. Just in case . . . things didn't work out in the end. Lily had spoken too soon, though, and she now had to explain herself.

"We promised that neither of us would see anyone else while we're apart," Lily explained quietly. "We promised to be true to each other." Lily frowned a little as she spoke. She remembered the exact moment when Jonathan had made her promise him. They were at the Maryland State Fair with the whole gang, having a wild, carefree time — everyone but Jonathan, who was his now-typically-uptight self. They'd been dancing to a country-rock band under one of the big tents, and right in the middle of a song the handsome lead singer had pulled Lily up onto the stage to dance out the number with him. It had been a delirious experience, and afterward the singer had given her a big kiss, making Lily the envy of all her female friends. It was completely harmless, but Jonathan had gotten green-eyed with jealousy. Lily could almost feel Jonathan's arms gripping her tightly. She could hear his earnest voice, making her promise not to date anybody else.

Stacy and Frankie were watching Lily, curious and concerned. "You look worried, Lily," Stacy said. "But you know you shouldn't be. Jonathan would never cheat on you — I'd bet anything he'll keep his end of the promise!"

"Yes, you know you can trust him," Frankie

affirmed. "He's definitely the faithful type. Sort of like Josh." She smiled and turned a little pink as she mentioned her boyfriend. "I have complete faith in Josh, and I think you should have the same in Jonathan."

"The same goes for Zack," Stacy declared with a confident toss of her ponytail. "I know he'd never let me down that way. Anyhow, I know where he is nearly every minute of the day. If he's not with me or in class, he's playing football!"

Lily smiled without responding. She knew her friends meant well, but they'd misinterpreted her discomfort about the promise. Lily smoothed the thin material of her dress down over her knees, stifling a small, dissatisfied sigh. She knew she should explain to Stacy and Frankie that it wasn't Jonathan she was worried about — it was herself. When they talked to her about how much Jonathan must miss her and how happy they were with their own boyfriends, Lily felt guilty. She would never have admitted it, but secretly, deep down in her heart, she was relieved that Jonathan was gone. Of course she missed him — and she definitely still loved him. But by the end of the summer, his anxiety and possessiveness had finally almost gotten the best of her. They couldn't go anywhere as a couple or do anything together without some sort of scene. All Lily had to do was look at another guy, much less talk to one, and Jonathan went through the ceiling. He didn't even like to share her with his own friends. And Lily was drained by Jonathan's constant demands on her emotions. He was always using her as a sounding board, bouncing off her all his doubts and fears about college, himself, and his future. It was only since he'd left for U Penn that Lily had regained all of her old drive, her spirit of fun, her ambition. She had the distinct feeling that if Jonathan had still been around, she wouldn't be at the Little Theater that very moment, waiting to try out for the fall play. She'd be too busy comforting him about one thing or another. She'd be Jonathan's girlfriend . . . instead of Lily Rorshack.

Lily continued to ponder her situation as Frankie and Stacy flipped through the *Twelfth Night* script, giggling over the old-fashioned Shakespearean expressions. When Jonathan had made her promise not to see other guys while they were separated, Lily had agreed. Even though the idea of such a promise bothered her, her love for Jonathan won out over her misgivings. Since then, though, her doubts about the promise had grown and grown. Lily had always valued her independence, and when she and Jonathan first started dating, she had thought he was as free-spirited as she was. She'd soon discovered differently. It was all a façade, and while she didn't think she loved Jonathan any less because of it, sometimes she missed the freedom of being unattached. In addition, while her relationship with Jonathan was the most serious one she'd ever had, they'd only known each other a few months. Lily wasn't certain that under the circumstances, such a blanket commitment was the right thing for either of them.

It's all so complicated! Lily thought to herself, squeezing her hands into small, tight fists inside the pockets of her loose-fitting cardigan. But she'd

25

made the promise and she would keep it. She wanted to — she loved Jonathan. And there wasn't any other guy she was interested in, at least not for the moment.

Although, Lily quickly remembered, she was always vulnerable to romance when she was acting in a play, especially if it was a play about falling in love like *Twelfth Night*, and *especially* if she was acting with a boy who was talented or good-looking or both. . . .

Lily jumped to her feet. "Hey, you guys," she called to Frankie and Stacy, "let's take a quick look at the list of people who are trying out before I go in and put my life on the line here." The other girls followed her to the wall where the names were posted. Lily scanned them quickly.

"Anyone you know?" inquired Stacy.

"Mm-hmm." Lily assented. "It looks like quite a few of the kids who were in *The Fantasticks* are auditioning, like Larry Hinson and Pete Mitchell."

"Do you think you have any real competition?" asked Frankie, counting the number of girls trying out.

"Well, you figure some of the girls will be interested in the role of Olivia — say that rules out half," Lily speculated, her head tipped to one side and one beaded earring brushing her shoulder. "There's definitely still some competition."

"What about those guys you mentioned?" Stacy, an incorrigible flirt despite her devotion to Zack, studied the boys' names curiously. "Are any of them cute?"

"Just so-so," Lily said. "I mean, I don't know

them all. There may be a Robert Redford or two in the bunch. We'll see!"

"Here's one." Stacy pointed at the list and giggled. "Buford Wod-jov-od-ski!" Frankie and Lily read the name in disbelief and then doubled over with laughter at Stacy's outrageous pronunciation. "Do you know ol' Buford, Lil?" Stacy asked.

"Nope," Lily admitted with a laughter-induced hiccup. "He didn't try out for *The Fantasticks*. I certainly would have remembered him if he did!"

"Well, he sounds like a heartthrob to me," Stacy said with a sly glance at her friends. "I bet he's five-feet-zero-inches tall and chubby, with glasses and a crew cut."

"No," Frankie contradicted in a firm tone. "He's at least seven feet tall and string-bean skinny, with size twenty shoes and a voice as high as Michael Jackson's!"

"You guys are terrible!" Lily whispered through her hiccups, looking around for an eavesdropping boy who fit either of these descriptions. "I'm sure Buford has a very nice . . . personality!"

After they recovered from their laughing fit, Stacy and Frankie sent Lily through the door to the theater, saying good-bye and telling her to break a leg. Lily closed the door behind her and walked down the aisle to the front of the theater, a smile still on her face. As she slid into a seat near the back of the group of students gathered to try out for the play, Mrs. Weiss, the new drama teacher, began explaining the audition procedure.

Lily listened carefully even as she thought to herself in amusement: If I'm going to be working on *Twelfth Night* with boys named Buford, it doesn't look as if I'll have too much of a problem staying true to Jonathan!

Chapter
3

Vince straightened up from his locker, looking nonchalantly around him as he tucked the loose tail of his red chamois shirt back into his jeans. Charlotte knew where his locker was — maybe she'd just happen to walk by on her way to the bus.

Vince shook this thought out of his head and closed his locker sadly. Char couldn't have made it any clearer the other morning on the quad. Roxanne was still standing between them, and Charlotte didn't want to have anything to do with him under any circumstances. The last thing in the world she was likely to do was "happen to walk by" his locker. It was foolish to hang around, waiting for that to happen. He'd be waiting until he graduated.

As he headed against the crush of departing students in the direction of the newspaper office, Vince flipped through his five-subject spiral notebook. On the last page was a carefully printed "Schedule of Events" for the Kennedy High Wilderness Club, of which Vince was president this year. Thanks to some ambitious fund-raising projects like selling corsages and boutonnieres at the prom the previous spring, the Wilderness Club had more money in its treasury than ever before. Activities for the year would include a weekend backpacking trip later that month, participation in a fire-fighting workshop sponsored by the Maryland Department of Natural Resources, cross-country skiing as soon as the first snow fell, and a rock-climbing expedition in the spring. It all sounded great to Vince, and he was psyched to lead the club. But he couldn't look forward to the backpacking trip, or anything else for that matter, as much as he would have if he'd thought there was a chance he'd be sharing the experience with Charlotte.

The door to the newspaper room was closed so Vince knocked. When nobody answered, he pushed the door open and peered in. The office of *The Washington Post* couldn't have appeared any more hectic. Daniel's desk was piled high with magazines, books, and papers. Daniel himself was hunched, scowling, over a typewriter, looking up only to holler something at one of his staff, who were all scribbling madly and looking generally frazzled. Vince smiled. That was Daniel, all right — as intense as they came. He'd probably turn out a first-rate newspaper, but he could easily burn himself out — and no doubt some of the other kids, too — in the process.

No one in the busy group heard Vince knock

or even seemed to notice him as he crossed the room to stand in front of Daniel's desk. Vince had to shout hello three times before Daniel tossed down his stubby pencil and looked up. The preoccupied expression partly faded from Daniel's face, and he greeted Vince with a half smile. "Hey, Mr. Wilderness! What brings you to my neck of the woods?"

Vince groaned at the pun. Ripping the schedule of events out of his notebook, he tossed it onto the desk. "I heard you didn't have enough to do so I brought you some more work to keep you out of trouble," he explained, dropping into an empty chair.

Daniel rubbed a hand across his eyes. "Gee, thanks, DiMase," he said sarcastically. "With friends like you. . . ! No, but seriously, let's see what you've got." Daniel gave the schedule a quick, professional glance and then nodded with approval. "It'll fit fine on the back page," he announced. "Thanks for putting it together so fast. Most of the club schedules'll probably be turned in at the last possible minute. Non-journalists just don't appreciate the importance of deadlines, you know?"

Vince raised his dark eyebrows, amused at Daniel's superior tone. "I can imagine," he said, holding back a grin. Just then, both he and Daniel were distracted by Sara Gates, who was on her way over. Vince didn't know much about Sara except that she was a junior and one of the new editors Daniel had spoken of so highly. Now Vince looked on curiously as Sara handed Daniel a neatly typewritten sheet and then stood aside,

31

fidgeting nervously with her tortoiseshell glasses while Daniel read over her work.

Vince wasn't sure what sort of comment he expected Daniel to make — some manner of praise, certainly, after the way he'd raved about Sara's work the other day. So when Daniel's forehead creased in a critical frown, Vince was surprised. He was even more surprised when Daniel gave Sara her paper back, dismissing her and it with a curt, "This isn't a movie review, Sara. This is a plot summary. That's not what I want for *The Red and the Gold*."

Sara took her review without a word, but Vince saw her bite her lip before she turned and walked quietly back to the worktable she shared with a few others in the rear of the office. Vince's jaw was still open in astonishment. He turned to his friend, a questioning expression on his face. "Hey, Tackett, don't you think that was a little rough?" Vince spoke forcefully. He hated to see anyone — especially a girl — treated unfairly, and that was exactly what Daniel had just done to Sara. "She looks like she's working as hard as anybody else around here, you included."

Daniel reddened slightly and then sighed, leaning forward with his elbows on the desk and his forehead resting on his palms. "I was a little tough," he acknowledged, his voice low.

Vince studied his friend's gloomy face, suddenly pretty sure he knew what was bothering him. "I don't mean to stick my nose in your business, buddy," he began cautiously. "But it kind of looks to me like maybe you're taking out some of your personal frustrations on your staff. Am I right?"

Daniel nodded, a shock of rebellious dark hair falling over his eyes. "Yeah, I suppose you're right," he admitted with some reluctance.

"Is it Lin?" Vince asked sympathetically.

Daniel nodded again. "What else?"

At the leadership conference that summer — the same fateful conference during which Vince had gotten to know Charlotte, while doing his best to make Roxanne understand that their romance was over — Daniel had met a beautiful girl from a downtown D.C. high school. They'd really seemed to hit it off, and Vince had assumed that Daniel and Lin would go out after camp was over. But it hadn't worked out that way. From what Daniel had told him, Lin's parents, Asian immigrants and very conservative, had not approved of Lin dating anyone — especially someone with a different background from theirs. For that reason Lin had broken off the relationship, unwilling to disobey her parents no matter how much she might like Daniel. Daniel had barely mentioned Lin since his last encounter with her, and now it struck Vince that maybe it would make his friend feel better to talk a little bit about what was bothering him. Anyone could see Daniel needed to let off steam.

"So, what's the story?" Vince prodded as discreetly as he could.

Daniel leaned back in his chair, folding his hands behind his head and trying to look nonchalant. "It's pretty basic," he said dryly. "I mean,

33

you know as much as I do, really. Her parents don't approve of me, and their word is the law." He gritted his teeth. "What kills me is that they — she — won't even give me a chance. I've called several times, and either her parents don't give her the message or Lin just doesn't want to return my calls. I'm not sure which would be worse!" Daniel's laugh was bitter. "That's the story, Vince, my boy. It's on the short side — not exactly TV-movie material. I don't really have any other choice but to pour myself into school and this newspaper. See what I mean?"

"Yeah." Vince sighed deeply. "I see, all right." He could see it only too well, actually. Vince wished he could talk his friend out of his funk, but he was the last person who'd be able to give Daniel positive advice. Wasn't he in a similarly depressing situation with Charlotte? Charlotte liked him, Vince was sure of it — just like Daniel and Lin. And as time went on, he saw less and less reason for his former romance with Roxanne to stand in the way. But if Charlotte refused to meet him halfway, there wasn't anything Vince could do about it. Yes, Vince could see Daniel's problem. Roxanne was as much of a brick wall between him and Charlotte as Lin's parents were between Lin and Daniel.

Vince got slowly to his feet, stretching his muscular arms over his head. There didn't seem to be much point in hanging around the newspaper office any longer. He hadn't had much success in cheering Daniel up — all he was doing was keeping him from his work. "Well, I'll see you around," Vince said, slapping Daniel lightly on the back. "Good luck with all this editorial stuff. I can't wait to see the first issue."

"It'll be worth waiting for," Daniel assured him. His dark eyes flickered. "Thanks for coming by with the schedule. Thanks for . . . everything."

Vince shrugged. "No problem. Any time you want to talk. . . ."

"Gotcha." Daniel waved good-bye and bent over his papers. Vince crossed the office, giving Sara Gates a comforting grin in passing. She smiled back weakly. Vince's grin faded, though, as he pulled the office door shut behind him and trudged slowly down the deserted hallway. As he entered the stairwell, his conversation with Daniel was still weighing heavily on his mind. He might criticize Daniel for taking out his personal frustrations on his staff, but Vince had to admit that there was something to be said for Daniel's fundamental drown-your-sorrows-in-your-work strategy. Maybe Daniel had the right idea, even if he took it to an extreme. Vince figured he could do worse than to follow Daniel's lead and put all *his* energy into activities like the Wilderness Club and the volunteer rescue squad he worked with. If doing that could take his mind off Charlotte DeVries, it just might be worth a try.

Roxanne turned a corner and strolled down the nearly empty corridor, her determined green eyes fixed on her destination: the office of *The Red and the Gold* at the far end of the hall. Suddenly she stopped in her tracks, her heart jumping painfully. A well-built, dark-haired boy had just emerged from the office and was walking away from her. A moment later he'd disappeared into the stairwell, but Roxanne couldn't fail to recognize Vince, even from a distance. The clunky hiking boots, the outdoorsy shirt, the long stride, the thick, wavy hair. . . . Roxanne swallowed the lump in her throat and went on her way with even more determination than before. Seeing Vince and being reminded of how much it had hurt her to lose him to Charlotte only made Rox's current errand twice as urgent.

Vince had left the door to the newspaper room slightly ajar, and Rox slipped inside inconspicuously. It only took a second to see that Jana Lacey, the reason for her visit, wasn't in the office. If everything Daniel had said about working his staff half to death was true, though, Jana couldn't be far away. Then Roxanne's curious gaze settled on Sara Gates, who was perched on a high stool at a big, paper-strewn table, busily scribbling away. Roxanne sniffed disdainfully. The fact that Sara was going out with her younger brother Torrey wasn't exactly a recommendation in Rox's eyes. Torrey might have cleaned up his act somewhat since he'd started going out with Sara, but he was still a delinquent, and therefore, as sweet and all-American as Sara might appear, she had to be as big a loser as the rest of Torrey's friends. Well, Rox could still buy some time by visiting for a few minutes with Sara. It wouldn't kill her to play the caring and concerned big sister this once.

Roxanne wove her way toward Sara, secretly relieved that Daniel, who had his back to her, hadn't seen her come in. Things could never be anything but tense between Roxanne and her former Stevenson ally. Not after last spring when, in the ultimate move of wimpy cowardice, Daniel had deserted Rox's anti-Kennedy camp to become one of "the crowd." Just because he lost the election for student government president to that preppy elitist Greg Montgomery. . . . With an effort, Roxanne pushed her ill feelings back down as far under the surface as they would go. She'd decided that it was in her best interest to adopt an if-you-can't-beat-'em-join-'em policy, but sometimes it was hard. But now for the business at hand. . . .

Tossing her long, sun-streaked red hair over one shoulder, Roxanne slipped onto the empty stool next to Sara. "Hi, Sara," she said in the friendliest tone she could manage. "You look awfully busy. What are you working on?"

Sara looked at Roxanne with surprise and undisguised distrust. Rox, not fazed in the least, flashed her a bright smile. Sara cleared her throat and her rosy cheeks turned a deeper pink. "I'm writing a movie review," she explained, covering the typed page, now scrawled with handwritten corrections, with one freckled hand.

Roxanne nodded, stifling a bored yawn. "All the time Daniel makes you spend in the newspaper office — I bet Torrey's jealous. How is everything between you two these days, anyway?"

Now Sara's voice became distinctly cool. "Everything's just fine, thanks," she said stiffly. Roxanne barely noticed the change. She couldn't have been less interested in Sara's work or her relationship with Torrey, and it must have shown because now Sara gave her a questioning look. "Are you looking for someone, Roxanne?"

Roxanne dug into her black snakeskin shoulder-bag and pulled out a crumpled piece of paper, her flimsy excuse for dropping by the office. "I wanted to deliver this yearbook news," she said, hoping she sounded official. She was a legitimate member of the yearbook staff, after all. Then Roxanne decided that there was really no reason not to come right out and tell Sara her true reason for being there. Sara couldn't possibly guess Roxanne's ulterior motive, and she might even be some help in the matter. "And actually," Roxanne added nonchalantly, "I was looking for Jana Lacey. Has she been around this afternoon?"

Sara nodded at a pile of papers across the table. "She's in the middle of writing an article. She couldn't have gone far. My guess would be she just went to the girls' room." Pointedly, Sara turned her attention back to her review.

Roxanne hopped off the stool and straightened the skirt of her short, tight jersey dress. Sara certainly seemed eager enough to get rid of her, but that was fine with Rox. She'd wasted enough time on Sara — and she'd gotten what she wanted from her. "Thanks, Sara," she said over her shoulder as she made a beeline for the door.

There wasn't a moment to lose — the bathroom would be a perfect place to corner Jana for a private chat. Roxanne hurried down the hall to the nearest girls' room and pushed open the door hopefully. Sure enough, there was Jana, pursing her lips in front of the mirror as she applied a fresh coat of fire-engine-red lipstick. Roxanne had never spoken with Jana before. She was seeking her out purely on the basis of her reputation as a champion gossip and a dedicated social climber. Now Rox took in the younger girl's appearance with a glance. Jana was very pretty. Her long, dark hair billowed around her shoulders, and her fluffy sweater and miniskirt showed off a curvy, compact figure. As she expertly glossed her lips, an armful of glittery bracelets clicked and clacked. Roxanne recalled what she'd heard about Jana's older brother, Peter. Supposedly Peter, who'd been a crack D.J. and manager of the Kennedy radio station, was incredibly good-looking. Wouldn't you know it, Rox thought, not for the first time. *I transferred to this stupid high school just in time to miss all the* real *men.* But at that moment she was more interested in Jana than in ten Peter Laceys. It was time to go to work.

Joining Jana in front of the mirror, Roxanne pretended to have wandered in by coincidence. She pulled her compact from her bag and dabbed delicately at her nose. Then she executed a smooth double-take. "You're Jana Lacey, right?" she said in a sweet, uncertain tone.

Jana turned to her in surprise. Roxanne was pleased to see that Jana plainly recognized *her* and seemed flattered at Rox's attention. "Yes, I am," Jana affirmed eagerly.

"Well, I've been hoping to run into you for ages," Rox gushed warmly. "I wanted to thank you for missing leadership camp over the summer. I got to go in your place, and I had the absolute greatest time!" It was true that Roxanne was able to participate in the conference only because Jana, who'd been chosen to attend, went to Europe on a summer exchange program instead, thereby opening up an extra space. What Rox neglected to mention, though, was that the conference was the worst week of her entire life. She'd publicly fallen flat on her face in all her schemes to get Vince back, and in the meantime Charlotte had been snaring him with her ultra-feminine wiles. Not only that, but during the final camp project Roxanne had gotten lost in the woods, twisted her ankle, and contracted a wicked case of poison ivy. Her misery had been complete.

Roxanne didn't want to bring up the topic of Charlotte just yet. She couldn't rush it. Jana had to be entirely unsuspecting. "Really," Roxanne continued, her eyes wide and earnest, "it was a fantastic opportunity. I learned so much! I'm only sorry you had to miss out, Jana. But I guess a summer in Europe doesn't exactly count as 'missing out.' "

Jana responded to Roxanne's glowing words and warm smile with a broad smile of her own. "No, Europe was fantastic. I wouldn't trade it for anything. But I'm so glad you enjoyed the conference."

Roxanne pushed the point. "It was educational, but it was also fun," she assured Jana. "A couple of other people from the crowd" — Rox carefully emphasized these last two words — "participated. I feel even more a part of things at Kennedy now because of it."

Roxanne was gratified to see that Jana had

40

taken the bait whole. At the mention of the crowd, the other girl's face had become more animated, almost hungry-looking. Rox knew that look. What she didn't realize was that she knew it so well because it mirrored so precisely the feelings she'd had herself for so long — the overpowering desire to *belong*. Now, thanks primarily to her friendship with Charlotte, Roxanne did belong, in a way. And there was no reason for Jana to know how tentative her hold on popularity was. She had Jana thinking she, Rox, held the key to something Jana wanted very badly. It suited Rox perfectly to just go on letting Jana think she could give it to her.

As if by an unspoken understanding, both girls now stashed their makeup and settled back for a chat, Rox hitching one hip up on the edge of a sink and Jana leaning back against the paper-towel dispenser. "I know Daniel considered the leadership conference a real success," Jana observed. "Although you've got me how they could have taught him anything he didn't already know about bossing people around!" Rox laughed and Jana shook her head. "Seriously, he's a slave driver. I'm not sure what I've gotten myself into with this newspaper stuff."

Roxanne fawned subtly. "Obviously Daniel made you an editor because you're a talented writer. I'm sure you're doing fine."

Jana smoothed her hair back from her face, looking self-satisfied. "Maybe," she said modestly. "You know, sometimes I think all Daniel's intensity over *The Red and the Gold* is just his way of taking out his disappointment at not being elected student government president. Not that he would have made as good a president as Greg Montgomery," Jana added with ardent conviction. Roxanne nodded rapturously, pretending to share Jana's idolatrous view of Greg. "Although I don't know how Greg can concentrate on running the student government," Jana rattled on, not missing a beat. "Did you know" — she lowered her voice conspiratorially, and Roxanne leaned forward, curious despite herself — "he actually taped a letter from Katie up inside his locker? Can you believe it? Anyway, apparently Katie loves college but she misses Greg like crazy. Well, who could blame her! Nope, there's no chance for the rest of us girls where Greg's concerned. Katie's still got him tied around her little finger. But then with Zack McGraw to fall all over, who'd mope about Greg?"

Roxanne marveled at the speed with which Jana switched gears. Now she proceeded to reel off the name of all the Kennedy females who were falling all over Zachary like lovesick puppies since he'd achieved hero status after the first football game. Roxanne's mind whirled. Jana was a veritable goldmine of gossip, even more so than Rox had expected. With absolutely no encouragement, Jana continued to feed her with tasty tidbits about various students — even the popular ones. It was amazing to Roxanne that Jana should possess so much personal information about people she didn't even know. But far be it from Roxanne to question any of it. She simply looked impressed and let Jana chatter herself out.

Finally Jana straightened up, seeming to realize that it was time to get back to the newspaper office. Drawing a brush from her pocketbook, she faced the mirror and gave her hair a quick brush. "Of course, Rox," she added as sort of a postscript to her revelations, "this is all *privileged* information."

Roxanne was all seriousness. "I won't tell another soul," she promised. She watched Jana tuck her hairbrush back in her purse and suddenly realized there wasn't a moment to lose. It was time to put the rest of her plan into action. Biting her lip as hard as she could, Roxanne managed to squeeze a few fake tears into her eyes. She wiped at them ostentatiously, drawing Jana's attention with the gesture.

"Why, Rox, what's the matter?" Jana asked, crossing to Roxanne's side and placing a hand on her arm. "You look upset."

"It's nothing," Rox sniffled, playing the martyr.

"There's something bothering you," Jana argued. "Come on, you can tell me."

"Well. . . ." Roxanne sniffled again, pretending to hesitate. Then she gave in. "It would be so nice to tell somebody who'd understand," she admitted in a small voice. "But first, Jana, you have to promise me, cross your heart, you won't tell *anyone.*"

Roxanne knew that the more she emphasized the need for secrecy, the more likely it was that Jana would leave the bathroom and tell Roxanne's story to the first person she saw. And that was exactly what Rox wanted. It was a promise made to be broken.

Jana's eyes sparkled with curiosity even as she swore her lips were sealed. "You can trust me not to tell a soul."

"Good." Roxanne heaved a deep, shaky sigh. "It's nice to know I can trust someone," she said self-pityingly. "I *thought* I could trust Char DeVries. I *thought* she was my best friend. Boy, was I wrong."

"You were?" Jana asked eagerly.

"Charlotte betrayed me." Roxanne blinked her eyes, as if more tears threatened. "She's a . . . she's a boyfriend-stealer!"

Rox colored her accusation with all the sorrow, disgust, and bitterness she could muster. Jana's eyes nearly popped out of her head. Rox wouldn't have been surprised if the other girl had licked her lips. It *was* a juicy morsel of dirt. But it was also the truth, after all. She wasn't telling Jana about Charlotte just to be catty. Char was a traitor and if, thanks to Jana, the whole high school soon knew that, it was no more than Charlotte deserved.

Jana's obvious interest and her own aching anger spurred Rox on in her recital. "I wish it wasn't, but it's the truth," she assured Jana. "I heard Char was positively famous at her old high school in Alabama for snagging all the attached boys." Roxanne couldn't refrain from embellishing her confession with a few out-and-out lies. They weren't terribly far from reality as far as Rox was concerned, and if they cemented the story more firmly in Jana's mind, so much the better. "She does it just for the fun of hurting people," Rox continued. "Once she gets a boy to like her, once she steals him away from the girl who really cares for him, she dumps him just like that and goes on to the next!"

"That's horrible!" Jana breathed, her gold-toned earrings jingling vigorously as she shook her head in outrage.

"Well, just look at Vince." A shadow of genuine pain darted across Roxanne's dark expression. "He . . . he broke up with me so he could sneak off with Charlotte at the state fair. Now Char will barely talk to him, and he looks miserable."

Jana seemed willing to swallow Roxanne's tale hook, line, and sinker, but there was clearly something standing in her way: her own positive impression of Charlotte. She furrowed her slender black eyebrows. "But Char seems so friendly, so sweet. . . ."

Roxanne squashed Jana's tiny doubt like a bug on a sidewalk. "Don't fall for that southern-belle routine, Jana," she urged the other girl. "Believe me, I've learned the hard way. Char's bubbly charm is just an act that covers up a first-class snake!"

Rox uttered this with such conviction that Jana wouldn't have questioned her for the world. She gave Rox a quick, comforting hug. "I'm sorry about what happened with Vince, Roxanne," she said. "Who would have thought someone we've trusted with so much responsibility at this school would turn out to be such a monster?"

Locating a tissue in her bag, Rox wiped the smudges of mascara from under her eyes. "Well, at least I wasn't the only one taken in by Charlotte.

45

All of Kennedy High thinks she's Miss America!"

"It's just not right." Jana shook her head. She was clearly bursting with eagerness to spread the news, but for Roxanne's benefit she repeated her vow of silence. "I'm glad you confided in me, Rox. And I promise I won't breathe a word of this to anyone."

"I know you won't," Rox said, smothering a triumphant smile. "Thanks a million for listening, Jana. Somehow, I feel better having shared this with you."

And I'll feel even better after you've shared it with everyone you know! Rox added silently to herself as she and Jana left the girls' room together.

Chapter
4

Lily shifted in her seat at the Little Theater. She was beyond antsy; she felt ready to jump out of her skin. Nearly all the boys interested in a part in *Twelfth Night* had auditioned. It seemed to Lily that there had been at least a hundred of them, but she knew that was only because she was so eager to audition herself. She tried not to think about the fact that Mrs. Weiss had run through the list of boys' names alphabetically. If she did the same for the girls, it could be another hour before Lily's turn came around. There was nothing to do but be patient, though, and Lily willed herself to relax as she sank back in her seat, her eyes on the stage.

Mrs. Weiss exchanged a few words with the boy who had just tried out and then checked her clipboard for the next name. This absolutely *has* to be the last guy to audition, Lily thought to herself hopefully. "Buford Wodjo-vod-ski . . ." Lily stifled a giggle as Mrs. Weiss stumbled over the mouthful. She had almost forgotten about good old Buford!

She leaned forward slightly, interested to see whether Stacy's or Frankie's description of him came closer to actuality. Actuality, however, made Lily's jaw drop. Buford Wodjovodski had been sitting a few rows in front of her the entire time she'd been in the theater, but she hadn't noticed him because of the dim lights. As he stepped onto the stage, however, Lily noticed him, and how. Buford was fairly tall — Frankie had guessed correctly there — but he wasn't skinny or geeky-looking. Instead, he was your basic gorgeous hunk, sort of arty in the way Lily always found irresistible. He had classically handsome features and thick dark hair that was a little bit long on top. His worn, faded jeans fit him well. Before he started in on his reading with Mrs. Weiss, Buford stripped off his leather jacket and white aviator scarf, revealing broad shoulders underneath a Folger Theater sweat-shirt.

Lily blinked once or twice, stunned. *That* was Buford Wodjowhat's-his-name? So much for being safe from the distraction of a cute — a very cute — guy in the cast! Despite herself, Lily was suddenly overcome by a misty vision of herself alone on the stage with Buford. It was a romantic scene and his arms were around her, their faces only inches apart. . . . The audience held its breath as they drew even closer for the climactic kiss. . . .

Lily shook her head sternly. Ridiculous! Not

48

only was her daydream disloyal to Jonathan, but for all she knew neither she nor Buford would get a part in the play. Well, she'd get a part. But even though Buford looked good, it was very possible he couldn't act for beans. Lily found herself hoping that this was the case. If she was cast, she'd feel safer if Buford wasn't.

But when Buford began reading, it was immediately apparent that he was as talented as he was good-looking. He'd chosen to read from a scene in *Twelfth Night* featuring the character Malvolio, Duchess Olivia's comically ambitious steward. As he read the lines, barely glancing at the script in his hand, Malvolio came alive in all his pomposity. Buford was confident and funny without falling prey to the cardinal sin of acting: *over*acting. He was a professional through and through. Lily wasn't the only person brought to the edge of her chair by Buford's audition. When he finished reading, there was a spontaneous scattering of applause in the Little Theater.

Lily sat back, breathless. Buford's audition had easily been the best so far that afternoon. Mrs. Weiss was sure to give him a good part. And that meant if *she* got a part, too. . . . As Buford crossed the stage and then hopped down into the aisle, Lily stared at him, suddenly feeling as though she'd seen him somewhere before. His face, his voice when he spoke on stage, the way he moved. . . . No, it wasn't possible. She would definitely have remembered meeting him. If nothing else, she would have at least remembered his name!

Now Mrs. Weiss started in on the girls' auditions. Quite a few girls whom Lily knew and liked from the Drama Club were trying out — Jeannie, Terry, Carla — and they all did a good job. Lily wished everyone the best, but that didn't stop her from evaluating their performances with a critical eye and feeling sure that she had a very good shot at the leading role herself. By the time Mrs. Weiss called her name, Lily was pumped to audition, the adrenaline making her toes and fingers tingle. She wasn't even distracted by Buford's striking profile as she passed the row in which he was sitting. Right now, nothing existed for Lily beyond the stage and the script.

Onstage, she showed Mrs. Weiss the scene she wanted to try, one in which Viola lectured Duke Orsino on the correct way to woo a lady. When the drama teacher gave her the cue to proceed, Lily only hesitated for a fraction of a second. Then she was reading, pouring all her emotional and physical energy into the character so that Viola's dialogue wasn't just words on a page but the speech of a living, breathing person. Lily didn't just read Viola, she *felt* Viola.

At the end of the scene, two pink spots of exertion on her pale cheeks, Lily looked to Mrs. Weiss for direction. There was a sparkle of approval in her eyes, but Mrs. Weiss was all business as she asked Lily to read briefly from another scene, this time as Countess Olivia. Then she thanked Lily, patting her on the shoulder as they walked together to the edge of the stage. Mrs. Weiss waved the next auditioner up and Lily trotted down the steps, hardly feeling her feet on the scuffed wooden boards. She was exhilarated from her audition and from the knowledge that she'd done well. She wished there was somebody waiting for her in the audience, one of her girlfriends or Jonathan even, anyone to share her excitement with. Oh, well, Lily thought carelessly, taking the next stair with an extra bounce.

Then all at once she noticed there *was* someone waiting for her, kind of. As she reached the bottom step, Lily found herself looking straight into Buford Wodjovodski's sky-blue eyes. Lily froze, her limbs suddenly feeling like they were made of marble. Buford's eyes found hers and his face broke into a smile. Lily smiled back with equal warmth. For the long moment that Buford held her gaze, they might as well have been the only two people in the theater.

Then Lily remembered herself — and her promise to Jonathan. She saw instantly that the only way to make sure she didn't break her vow was to steer clear of Buford, to never even so much as talk to him. It was hard to set such a rule for herself when Buford's eyes and smile were so friendly and inviting, but Lily knew she had to do it.

Lily didn't realize that Buford's glance had melted her knees and stopped her in her tracks at the foot of the aisle until he started to rise from his seat, still smiling at her, as if to approach her and begin a conversation. Lily's legs came back to life. She literally sprinted up the aisle. Buford didn't stand a chance of flagging her down. Ducking into the row where she'd left her coat and books, Lily grabbed them and then left the theater.

51

"Lily, phone!"

Her mother's raised voice drifted out to Lily, who was sitting on the back porch with her feet tucked up underneath her and an open biology textbook on her lap, rocking gently on the wooden swing. Lily snapped the book shut and jumped to her feet. She hadn't been reading anyway; the last few rays of the setting sun were too faint to see by. She'd just been thinking — about Buford. Well, not really *about* Buford. After all, she didn't even know him. It was more the idea of Buford that was on her mind, and what that idea might mean for her and Jonathan.

Mrs. Rorshack held the receiver out to Lily with one hand, shutting the oven on a steaming casserole with the other. Lily put the phone to her ear and said a cheery hello, expecting it to be Stacy or Frankie on the other end, checking in to hear about her audition. Instead, it was Jonathan. Pulling the phone cord around the corner into the dining room, Lily blushed as if she'd been caught doing something wrong. Would he be able to tell by the tone of her voice that she'd just been thinking about another boy? "Uh, hi, Jonathan! What a surprise!" Lily said, forcing some enthusiasm into her voice. She *was* surprised, although she knew she shouldn't be. These days, nine out of ten of her phone calls were from Jonathan.

"How're ya doing, Lil?" Jonathan's loving tone made Lily feel a pang of quilt. "I've been thinking about you all day." He laughed. "I mean, even more than usual. How were the tryouts for the fall play?"

The auditions were the last thing Lily wanted to talk about right then, but she was cornered. "They were fine," she said casually. "I'm pretty sure I'll get a part."

"Pretty sure?" Jonathan repeated, teasing. "Come on, Rorshack! You know as well as I do you're the most talented actress at Kennedy. Their only problem is going to be deciding which part to give you since they probably wish they could have you play them all!"

Jonathan's pride and belief in her sent a warm wave of affection rushing through Lily. She pressed the receiver closer to her cheek, suddenly wishing she were holding Jonathan instead of the phone. After all, he might not be perfect, he might even annoy her sometimes, but she was incredibly lucky to have such a devoted boyfriend. No one could be more caring, more interested in her and her life. "Thanks, Jonathan," Lily said softly.

"Hey, it's just the truth," he assured her. "But seriously, Lil. Do you think you'll get Viola?"

"I have a good chance," she admitted, twirling the phone cord around her finger.

"Well, you'd better. I've already marked my calendar, and I plan to be at every performance."

Lily laughed. "Well, in that case. . . ."

"There's just one thing, though. You'd better not have to kiss anybody as part of your role! I wouldn't stand for it, not for a minute."

Jonathan said it playfully, but Lily knew him well and she detected the serious, jealous note underneath the teasing. She hastened to reassure him as she always did at these moments, but for the first time with an odd feeling of insincerity. "Don't worry. There's not much kissing in Shakespeare. Back in those days the female roles were played by boys, remember?"

Jonathan laughed heartily. "Glad to hear it!" he said. Lily could tell he meant it.

She was eager to change the subject. "So, enough about me. What's new with you, Mr. Big Man on Campus?"

Jonathan sighed and Lily knew what was coming. She'd heard the same story every day since Jonathan left for school on the first day of September. "Not much is new," he began, his voice settling into a discouraged drone. "I mean, everything's new but nothing's *new*, you know? Classes are fine. The dorm is fun — there are some nice guys on my hall. I just wish you were here to share it with me. I miss you, Lil — I even miss Kennedy, just because you're there. I seriously would have done another year of high school if I could."

Lily knew he would have and could only breathe a sigh of relief that he hadn't. "I miss you, too, Jonathan," she responded, somewhat flatly. A minute earlier she *had* missed him, but now the pressure of his demanding emotions had squashed some of her tender feelings. Lily glanced up. Her mother was signaling at her from the kitchen with a wooden spoon. "Sorry to cut you off, but it looks like dinner's ready," Lily informed Jonathan without regret. "I'll talk to you again soon, though."

"I'll call you tomorrow," Jonathan promised.

Lily swallowed a sigh. "Okay. 'Bye, Jonathan."

"I love you, Lily," he said wistfully.

"Love you, too."

Lily followed the cord back into the kitchen and replaced the phone. Her thoughts were busy as she hurried to set the table while her mom, dad, and brother brought out the casserole, a huge bowl of salad, and the milk pitcher. Jonathan hadn't once mentioned their vow about not seeing other people, but it had been on Lily's mind during the entire conversation, and she knew he'd been thinking about it, too. There was just no getting away from it.

And there was no getting away, either, from the fact that the rule she'd made that afternoon about not talking to Buford was even more important than ever. Buford represented a temptation Lily had to resist if she wanted to keep her relationship with her boyfriend intact. Nope, she'd made a rule — and she planned to keep it.

Chapter
5

"And when Zack did that quarterback fake thing where he just pretended to hand off the ball and then ran all the way down the field for a touchdown? Josh and I jumped up and down for about twenty minutes. I almost fell off the bleachers I was so excited!"

Frankie laughed as she recounted the incident, and Stacy beamed proudly. "It looked pretty good from where I was standing, too," Stacy admitted, dunking a french fry in some ketchup. "That's one of the great things about cheerleading. You're practically on the field with the football players!" She smiled impishly. "About ten times during the game, the other girls had to hold me back from running out to give Zack a hug."

Stacy, Frankie, and Lily were comfortably settled in a roomy booth at the rear of the sub shop, a popular after-school and weekend hangout for many Kennedy students, and their friends in particular. It was a casual restaurant, the kind of place where kids felt comfortable because it was as cluttered as their own bedrooms. University banners and baseball pennants fluttered from the rafters, and in the four corners of the large room lurked four strange figures: a life-sized wooden Indian, a stuffed bear, a genuine moose head, and an antique jukebox which was now pouring forth John Cougar Mellencamp's latest hit.

The three girls were enjoying a big lunch in anticipation of a Saturday afternoon shopping spree. In between bites they replayed the action of the previous night when the Kennedy High football team trounced Leesburg Military Academy, traditionally their fiercest sports rival. Nearly every Kennedy student had been on hand to see Zack lead the way to victory with three touchdown passes and a touchdown of his own. As a result, Zack's status as school hero was now firmly established. In fact, at the party after the game, Stacy had barely had a chance to talk or dance with him. He'd been too besieged by people wanting to congratulate him, slap him on the back, and go on and on about what a great game he'd played. Of course he'd eaten up the attention, and who could blame him? Certainly not Stacy. She was as proud of Zack's triumph as he was. Besides, after last spring's gymnastics season, she knew how exciting it was to be in the spotlight. Stacy was all for Zack making the most of the fun while it lasted.

Frankie took a hefty bite of her Italian sub and chewed it carefully. Then she waved the sub at Stacy. "I don't know, though, Stacy," she said, teasing now. "I mean, it's all well and good to be going out with the Man of the Hour, but give me Mr. Low-Key any day! I like good old Josh just the way he is. What I mean is, you're not going to have Zack all to yourself anymore. The problem with dating a football star is that everybody wants him!" Frankie almost blushed, recalling her long-time crush on the super jock.

"Yeah, have you noticed lately," Lily chimed in, wiggling her eyebrows suggestively, "how everywhere Zack goes he's followed by a herd of adoring females? I bet the guy can't even get any privacy in the bathroom!"

Stacy frowned. "It's not that bad. . . ." She wrinkled her nose. "Is it?"

" 'Fraid so," Lily apologized. "I think gorgeous groupies just come with the territory."

It hadn't occurred to Stacy to be nervous about Zachary's sudden popularity, but now, even though she knew her friends were joking, she suddenly saw it in a new light. Zack *was* turning heads — female heads — like crazy these days. It was even worse than usual. That would probably be a temptation for any boy, even a loyal sweetheart like Zack.

Frankie noticed that Stacy really looked worried. "Stacy, we were only kidding you," she said reassuringly as she leaned across the table to steal one of Lily's onion rings. "I mean, Zack *is* currently Kennedy's number one heartthrob, but I don't think you should feel threatened. After all, he's *your* boyfriend."

"And he's not the kind of Don Juan who goes

wandering from one bimbo to the next, is he?" added Lily.

Stacy shook her head, her hair fanning out over her shoulders. "No . . . no, he's not." She hesitated. Then she pictured Zack at the party the night before. At one point they'd been separated by well-wishers, and he'd caught her eye above the sea of people. He'd raised on eyebrow as if to say, Can you believe this baloney? Stacy laughed out loud. "No, he's not a wanderer," she concluded firmly. "I can trust him totally."

"I'm sure you can." Frankie took a sip of her strawberry milk shake and then smiled. "But I'm still glad it's not Josh who's the local hero!"

Stacy shrugged carelessly. "I'd like to think that this attention will be all over once football's over . . . but he's good at *all* sports!"

Lily threw a french fry at her, laughing. "Some girls have all the luck!"

"Oh, I knew I had something I wanted to tell you guys!" Stacy suddenly exclaimed, bending down to retrieve her battered leather handbag from under the table. "Actually I have something to *show* you," she amended as she waved a pale green envelope. "A letter from Katie! She said a special 'hi' to both of you, so I thought you might like to read it."

Lily skimmed the letter first and then handed it to Frankie. "It really sounds like she loves Florida, huh?" she observed. "Although, who could blame her? Imagine — sunshine year round, palm trees outside your window, tanned hunks everywhere — I could handle that!"

"Too bad Katie's not interested in tanned hunks," Frankie pointed out. "Here she spends almost half a page going on and on about how much she misses Greg!"

"True," Lily conceded. "He probably doesn't have to worry about her cartwheeling off into the sunset with some lifeguard. Anyway, Katie's the one who should worry. Here's Greg, student body president, captain of the crew team, and just about the most visible person on campus with the exception of you-know-who." She winked at Stacy. "And half of those student bodies are female. These days Greg's a prime target for girls on the prowl!"

"Well, while I'm keeping an eye on Zack I can keep the other one on Greg," Stacy joked. "I'll keep Katie posted on all his 'extracurricular' activities."

As she passed the letter back to Stacy, Frankie checked her watch. "What do you suppose is holding up Char and Roxanne?" she wondered. "They said they'd be here by one and it's already quarter to two."

"Hmmm. I don't know." Stacy turned in her seat to look toward the front of the sub shop, but Charlotte and Roxanne were nowhere in sight. "Funny, it doesn't seem like Roxanne to be late for a shopping date!"

Lily sniffed. "Whose idea was it to invite her along, anyway?" she asked, making a sour face.

"Well, when I called Char about getting together, she said she already had tentative plans with Rox. So I suggested they both come," Stacy explained. She lifted a french fry to her mouth

60

and a small blob of ketchup splattered on the sleeve of her Coca-Cola sweatshirt. "Shoot!" She grabbed a paper napkin and, dipping it into a glass of ice water, began dabbing at the spot. "I mean, don't you think that was the right thing to do? You want to see Char, don't you?"

"Yes." Lily twirled a strand of dark blonde hair around one of her fingers, still looking doubtful. "But Rox — Well, *you* know. . . ."

Stacy did know. All three of the girls had gone to Stevenson with Roxanne before transferring to Kennedy, and they were familiar with her exploits, past and present. Stacy had never had much close contact with Roxanne herself, but she'd heard all the details of Frankie's and Lily's experiences with her. Frankie had been friends with Roxanne since childhood, but it had been a one-sided relationship with all the loyalty on Frankie's side. Roxanne had used Frankie, never letting Frankie emerge from her shadow long enough to become a person in her own right. It wasn't until they transferred and Frankie broke away from Roxanne that she came out of her shell. At Stevenson, Stacy had never even noticed Frankie.

Frankie had confirmed a story about Roxanne that had circulated around Kennedy the previous spring. In an attempt to snag as many boys at her new high school as possible, Rox had coerced Frankie into tampering with a special student government-sponsored computer Valentine service. As a result, Roxanne was "matched" with four different guys instead of getting the single date to which she was entitled. It had all blown up in her face at the Valentine's

Day Dance, though, when the boys involved discovered their dream date was being shared four ways.

As for Lily, Stacy knew she had a very good reason to be bitter toward Roxanne. Rox had helped stir up trouble between the Stevenson and Kennedy kids, and Stacy knew Lily held Roxanne responsible for all the misunderstandings that had been fostered early last year.

But the fact was, like it or not, they were stuck with Roxanne. They might as well make the best of it. "If we want Char, we have to take Rox, too," Stacy said. "And besides, if she's good enough for Charlotte, I for one, am willing to put up with her. I mean, we're just going *shopping*. We don't have to spend the rest of our lives with her."

"You've got a point," admitted Lily. "I really do like Char. She's so much fun to be with. Maybe she'll help keep our minds off Roxanne."

Frankie nodded. "Charlotte is great. Nothing stops her. I've never seen anybody who could get so much done in so little time. I really think as the new student activities director she's going to give Jonathan's reputation a run for the money!"

"She's the best," Stacy agreed sincerely. "I guess that's why I'm thinking maybe Rox isn't so bad after all. I mean, if a girl like Charlotte would accept her as a best friend. . . . And those two have been inseparable since summer." Stacy turned to Frankie to ask her opinion. "What do you think about Rox? After all, you know her practically better than anyone. Do you think she's really capable of turning over a new leaf?"

Frankie tipped her head to one side, thinking. "Six months ago I'd have said I wouldn't trust Roxanne under any circumstances. She let me down time and time again, and I just couldn't bring myself to believe in her anymore. But maybe she's changing. She has seemed different lately — quieter, a little more serious." There was a hopeful note in idealistic Frankie's voice. "Maybe she learned from her mistakes and is really trying to be a better person."

Lily continued to look skeptical. "You always look for the good side of people, Frankie. I'm just not so sure Roxanne has one!"

"Maybe we should give her the benefit of the doubt," Frankie suggested gently.

"You're right," declared Stacy. "Rox deserves yet another chance."

"Okay, okay! But I still want to see this snake's other skin," Lily said with a wicked twinkle in her eyes.

Fifteen minutes later Roxanne and Charlotte still hadn't arrived, and the three girls were beginning to get anxious. Stacy started to stand up, intending to call Char's house from the pay phone, but she didn't make it out of the booth. Jana Lacey had just swept into the sub shop and spotted Stacy, Frankie, and Lily from the door, and now she invited herself to join them. Stacy's escape route was effectively blocked as Jana slid in next to her.

Stacy caught Lily's eye across the table and grimaced slightly. This wasn't the first time that Jana had barreled in on them. Whenever the crowd was hanging out at the sub shop, which was pretty often since it was their favorite gathering place, chances were Jana would stop in and stroll by their table. Usually there wasn't a seat to spare, but today they had plenty of space in their enormous booth — unfortunately — Stacy couldn't help thinking.

"Well, hi!" Jana greeted them enthusiastically. Her trademark armload of bracelets jingled with her every move. "What are you three up to today?"

Lily had a sudden mischievous urge to make up a wild story for Jana. She wanted to say, "Oh, we're just grabbing a snack before we head to the National Gallery in D.C. to 'borrow' a few paintings to brighten up our bedrooms." Lily looked at Stacy and saw that her friend was thinking along the same lines. Instead she just smiled and answered, "We're up to lunch and some shopping later. A truly energetic Saturday."

Jana nodded, clearly not finding this tidbit terribly interesting. But when Frankie added, "We're waiting for Charlotte and Roxanne — they should be here any minute now," Jana's deep green eyes flashed. She bent forward, planting her elbows firmly on the table, her expression conspiratorial. The other girls all leaned toward her as if drawn by an irresistible magnetic force.

Jana started speaking, her voice low and loaded with hidden meaning. "I know all of you are . . . 'friends' with Charlotte, and that's why I especially wanted to talk to you." Jana's voice dropped even further, to a dramatic whisper. "I have something *very* important to tell you, but you can't tell anybody else. I wouldn't say a word

64

at all except you're all in danger, and I feel it's my duty to warn you!"

Jana's dire words caused Frankie, Stacy, and Lily to all exchange amused, skeptical glances. It was obvious they were about to be treated to some of her prize-winning gossip.

Stacy was half ready to laugh it off, but at the same time there was something genuinely gripping about Jana's urgent and uncharacteristically serious tone. Jana glanced around them as if to make sure they wouldn't be overheard. She brushed a strand of glossy black hair back from her face and took a deep breath. "Watch out for your boyfriends," she intoned darkly. Stacy lifted her eyebrows, surprised. Jana continued, "You might not believe this, but Charlotte DeVries stole the boyfriend of every friend she had in Alabama. What's worse, though, she didn't do it because she liked the boys necessarily — she did it just for sport. Then, once she had snared them, she broke the boys' hearts so badly that one of them actually had a kind of nervous breakdown and had to drop out of school!" Sensitive Frankie gasped at this, her eyes wide with shock. Even Lily shifted uncomfortably in her seat. Stacy, meanwhile, was riveted.

Jana sat back on the bench, sure now of her power over her listeners. "They say a leopard can't change its spots, and it doesn't look like Charlotte's changed hers since she moved to Rose Hill," she declared. "She's already playing the same game here! Her first victim was Vince DiMase. Has anyone noticed how depressed he's been lately?" The other girls nodded in unison.

"Well, I have it on the best authority that Charlotte first started in on him at leadership camp, just when he was on the verge of a reconciliation with Roxanne. Then at the state fair, Char lured him away from the rest of the gang, just to seduce him. And as soon as she'd hooked him, she dropped him like a rock!" Jana concluded her tale, still whispering self-righteously. "I'm only sharing this information with you because I don't want to see people get hurt. And I can't help suspecting the *real* reason Charlotte is spending time with you." Jana looked at Frankie and then rested her eyes sympathetically on Stacy. Stacy felt her face flood with color.

Before Stacy could ask Jana exactly what she meant by her last remark — even though she thought she knew — Jana slapped a hand over her mouth and, with a clatter of enameled bracelets, pointed toward the door of the sub shop with her other hand. All three girls followed the direction of Jana's pink-polished fingernail. Roxanne and Charlotte were standing in the doorway, busily scanning the dark restaurant. When Char's eyes came to rest on their table, she waved cheerily. Then she mimed something about a car and a phone call, and with Rox at her side, headed for the pay phone.

Jana was already halfway out of the booth. "I've got to run," she informed the others breathlessly. "*Promise* you won't breathe a word of this to anyone!" A moment later, Jana had scurried off to the sub shop take-out counter.

Lily shook her head, disbelieving. "Did we just hear what I think we heard?" she asked.

Frankie's forehead was wrinkled in a puzzled frown. "I just can't believe that Charlotte would — "

"Whoa, wait a minute," Stacy interrupted, waving her hands like a ref at a football game. She wasn't sure she believed Jana. She sure didn't *want* to believe her, for her own sake as much as for Charlotte's. If Char had her eye on Zack. . . . "What we heard isn't necessarily true! We all know Jana is a one-woman rumor machine. On any given day she probably tells enough sensational stories to fill a whole issue of the *National Enquirer*."

Frankie remained quiet. She wasn't sure what to think. Frankie knew that Charlotte didn't cause Roxanne and Vince's breakup, because she was there when Vince found out about the *real* Roxanne, at least the old Roxanne. No one else knew the reason why Vince was suddenly cool to Rox, and Frankie didn't intend to tell anyone their secret. She was too good a friend to betray confidences. But as far as Roxanne and Vince reconciling their relationship at leadership camp, Frankie had no idea about that. She'd hardly spoken to Roxanne all summer. It was possible that Rox and Vince *were* getting back together when Charlotte. . . .

"Char and Vince *did* disappear at about the same time at the state fair," recalled Lily.

"And Vince *has* been acting pretty down since school started," Stacy had to acknowledge. The evidence was fairly solid, and very upsetting. "Do you really think — Ow!"

Stacy's question was cut off by a sharp kick in

the shin from Lily. Rox and Charlotte were approaching, weaving their way among the closely spaced picnic tables. Char started apologizing before she'd even reached the booth. "I'm so sorry we're late!" she exclaimed. "You all must hate us!" Char collapsed on the bench next to Stacy while Roxanne hung their coats on a nearby rack. "First the VW broke down, that old bomb. We had to wait for the auto club to come and tow it to a gas station. Then we walked the whole way here from the station!" Charlotte's cheeks were still flushed from the exertion. "At least it's a nice fall day, just right for exercise! Although" — she bent over to peer ruefully at her pumps — "I didn't exactly wear my hiking shoes. Anyway, I just called my mom and she said not to worry, just to leave the car at the garage and go ahead and shop." Char paused to take a breath, not seeming to notice Frankie, Stacy, and Lily's silence. "And now I am absolutely starving. Aren't you, Rox? I know you've eaten, but could I hold up our expedition a few more minutes to grab some lunch?"

When the other girls nodded dumbly, Charlotte twisted in her seat, hunting for a waiter. She spotted one a few tables away, a cute boy who'd graduated from Kennedy the year before. Stacy, Lily, and Frankie stared as Char flirtatiously summoned him over and then, her long eyelashes fluttering, asked him in a low, confiding voice about the day's specials.

The waiter departed with Char's and Roxanne's orders. Lily, Frankie, and Stacy continued to stare. Suddenly Char seemed to realize that they were looking at her as if she were a ghost. "Hello, hello there!" she called, waving a hand playfully. "Is something the matter? You know, I really am sorry about keeping you waiting. I feel terrible. I should have called, but it didn't even occur to me, I was so flustered about the car. Forgive me?"

Stacy snapped out of her trance first. "Of course, Char," she assured the other girl with a weak smile. "We're all right. Just a little slow and sub-logged, that's all."

"Take your time. Enjoy your lunch," Frankie urged Charlotte, her fair skin unusually pale.

"You certainly couldn't help it if your car broke down," said Lily, not quite meeting Charlotte's eyes.

"Well, thanks for putting up with me," Char said, apparently satisfied with their answers. Just then the good-looking waiter arrived with Char's milk shake. She thanked him with a smile that sent a cold shiver up Stacy's spine.

Roxanne hadn't said a word since she'd sat down. Now she glanced in the direction of the take-out counter, her catlike eyes hungry. Sure enough, there was Jana Lacey, taking a paper bag from the cashier and heading with it for the door. Roxanne looked covertly at Lily, Stacy, and Frankie. It was all she could do not to cheer with satisfaction. Charlotte might not be picking up the tense vibes, but to Roxanne they were unmistakable. It looked like Jana had done her work splendidly. Rox bit back a smug smile, picked up her fork, and dug into her chef's salad with gusto.

Chapter
6

Lily's heart was galloping as she watched the clock over the door in Room 201. Her American history teacher droned on, oblivious to the fact that the entire class was poised on the edge of their seats, ready to bolt the instant the bell rang. Today Lily was especially eager for school to end. By now the casting results for *Twelfth Night* would be posted at the Little Theater. The first rehearsal was already scheduled. In just a few minutes she'd know if she'd won a role.

Two minutes . . . one minute . . . ten seconds. . . . Lily was on her feet and halfway out the door before the last bell of the day stopped ringing. She didn't bother stopping at her locker to get her books and coat — she could get them later since she had to catch the late bus home anyway.

Reaching the main lobby, Lily didn't have much choice but to let herself be swept up in the swirl of departing students. She hardly needed to move her own feet; the motion of the crowd carried her outside and deposited her in front of a row of parked school buses. Lily paused for a moment, crossing her arms over the front of her baggy purple sweater. It was a cold fall day and the low gray sky threatened rain. Lily shivered, oppressed by a sudden sensation of gloom. What if she reached the Little Theater only to discover that her name was nowhere on the list? It would be too terrible. But she had to find out, one way or the other. Lily dashed across the campus, not slowing down until she was at the Little Theater door.

The theater lobby was deserted except for two other students, who were walking away from the wall where the list hung. They passed Lily as she entered. It wasn't hard for Lily to guess that the boy on the left, his forehead creased with disappointment, hadn't gotten a role while the boy on the right, unable to restrain a victorious grin, obviously had. Which expression would she be wearing in a moment?

Lily pressed her damp palms against the hips of her short, checked skirt and approached the list. Another step and she'd be close enough to decipher the words. There was VIOLA right at the top . . . and her own name directly opposite it! She'd been cast in the leading role!

"All right!" Lily whooped, twirling around in a little dance. Then she leaned forward and gave the wonderful sheet of paper a spontaneous kiss. She'd dreamed, she'd hoped, she'd even secretly half-expected to be Viola, but she hadn't been certain. The knowledge that she *was* Viola filled her with a proud sense of accomplishment and anticipation. I'm Viola, Lily thought, her imagination taking flight. She pictured herself on stage, disguised in the boy's clothes Viola wore throughout the play; she heard her voice reaching out into the packed theater; she felt the heat of the lights and smelled that distinctive musty scent that always seemed to linger in the costumes and props.

Lily could have stood there all day, imagining scene after scene. Instead, she blinked her eyes a few times and focused again on the list, her excitement giving way to curiosity about the rest of the cast. She didn't realize she was looking for Buford Wodjovodski's name until she located it on the sheet. Not surprisingly, he had been cast in the central comic part of Malvolio, the most important male role in the play. A small sigh of relief escaped her. Lily blushed slightly, but she couldn't deny to herself that she was glad that Buford had been cast. She was also glad in a different way that he wasn't playing the smaller role of Orsino, the only boy in the play Lily, as Viola, might have to kiss.

"Congratulations, Lily! Or should I say congratulations, Viola?" Lily spun around, her dark blonde hair swinging in a startled arc. The deep male voice, resounding in the empty lobby, had just about shaken her out of her black leather boots. Lily's knees rattled a bit, too, when she found herself staring up into the owner of the voice's heart-stoppingly handsome face.

Buford smiled down at Lily, one dimple flashing. "Sorry. I didn't mean to scare you." He held out his right hand. "By the way, I'm Buford Wodjovodski. It looks like we're going to be spending some time together over the next few weeks!"

Lily lowered her eyes, suddenly feeling shy. She looked down wonderingly at Buford's outstretched hand. It was a few seconds before it occurred to her that he was holding it out by way of an introduction and she was supposed to shake it. Blushing, she took his hand. He gave her hand a warm squeeze and then dropped it casually. Lily glanced up at Buford again. Her mouth had gone as dry as sandpaper, and she was starting to worry whether she was capable of responding to Buford's remark. But now, as she met his eyes, the straightforward, friendly expression there made her nervousness melt away. In control again, Lily plopped down in one of the chairs in the entryway. "Congratulations yourself, Buford!" she said with a bright smile. "I bet you'll have a good time with Malvolio. I personally think he's a scream."

Buford nodded enthusiastically as he drew the other chair closer to Lily's until they touched. "I'm psyched," he admitted. "It's the role I wanted, and I was pretty sure I'd get it, but you never know. It'll be a kick."

Lily smiled. She liked Buford's self-confidence. He sounded positive about himself and his talents, but his attitude somehow didn't seem at all conceited. He was just being up front, and that was a characteristic Lily had always admired. "Well, from what I saw at auditions, you'll be a great Malvolio," she said sincerely.

"Thanks." Buford's eyes sparkled with appreciation. "And *you'll* be a perfect Viola. You have just the right quality on stage. A little bit of magic and mystery along with the spunk and sweetness, you know? That's what it takes to make Viola and her disguise really work."

Lily could feel her face flush from Buford's compliment. She herself thought she had a handle on an effective interpretation. But had Buford really been able to see all that in her five-minute tryout the other day? "I think I can do all right with Viola," she said, shrugging modestly. "It's a big step from the audition to the play itself, though."

Buford flicked a strand of sun-bleached blond hair back from his eyes and grinned. "Not for you," he insisted with authority. "You're special, Lily. And I'm not just talking about your audition. I remember you from *The Fantasticks* last spring. You stole the show. Seriously!"

Lily's eyes widened in surprise. She was amazed to hear that Buford had seen her in *The Fantasticks*, and what's more, remembered her. She was sure she'd never seen him around Kennedy before. Not only that, but there was something a little bit eerie and ironic about his choice of words. Jonathan had said practically the same thing to her after seeing the play himself last spring. You stole the show. . . . The memory gave Lily a brief twinge of guilt. A very brief twinge. It was literally impossible to think about anything — or anyone — else for very long when Buford was sitting only inches away from her with one of his muscular arms resting on top of the chair just behind her back.

"You remember me from *The Fantasticks*?" Lily asked, raising one dark blonde eyebrow. "But I played the mime role. I didn't have any lines, and I wore so much makeup my own family didn't recognize me!"

They laughed together, oblivious to the other students who were wandering in and out of the theater to find out the casting results. "I definitely remember you," he assured her, his eyes twinkling. Then the twinkle changed to an intense gleam. "I love the theater. No, I don't just love it, I'm crazy about it! I never forget a play, a scene, a role — or the actor or actress who performed it."

Lily was awed by the reverence with which Buford spoke about the theater. She loved it, too. In fact, she dreamed of some day being a stand-up comedienne and making the theater her career. But there was something different in Buford's attitude, something that made her own feelings seem a little bit amateurish in comparison.

Buford's emotions were genuine, Lily knew, but there was still one thing that puzzled her. "If you're so interested in acting," she began, tipping her head to one side, "and you're obviously talented, how come you haven't been in any other Kennedy productions recently? I'm one of the Stevenson transfers but I know you weren't in any plays last semester at least."

There was an odd sort of amusement in Buford's half smile. He looked as if he knew that he'd have to astonish Lily in order to answer her. "It's true, I haven't been in any Kennedy productions recently," he granted. "The last play I did here was about a year ago, I guess. Before you transferred. I didn't have time to try out for *The Fantasticks*, among other things, because I was in a play at the Folger at the time."

Buford made this statement without fanfare, but his words hit Lily like rocks falling into a pond, *kerplunk*. The Folger! A professional Shakespeare theater in Washington, D.C., the Folger was one of the most famous in the country. In addition to the theater itself, it also housed one of the largest collections of Shakespeare's works in the world. In Lily's eyes, the Folger *was* Shakespeare. And Buford had acted there, and now he was going to act in the Kennedy production, right alongside her! Lily's jaw had dropped, and now she was looking at Buford with as much surprise and admiration as if he'd just told her that he'd missed out on the last few Kennedy plays because he'd been in Hollywood accepting an Oscar. She was fascinated, but not too fascinated to be aware in the back of her mind that by talking to Buford like this — or rather by *enjoying* talking to Buford — she was sort of breaking the rule she'd set for herself the other day, the rule about avoiding contact with Buford and thereby avoiding being disloyal to Jonathan. To be on the safe side, maybe she should cut this discussion short right now. But then again, Buford was a professional actor, and she was sitting right next to him! Lily was dying to hear in depth about his experience at the Folger. Rule or no rule, she decided, she wasn't going to budge.

"You were in a play at the Folger?" Lily was practically shouting, she was so excited. "I can't believe it! That's amazing! I'm so envious. I can't imagine what it would be like to act in a *real* play. What play was it? How did you get a role there? Have you been in any other professional productions?"

Buford laughed at Lily's rapid-fire questions. "It's really not that big a deal," he insisted with a nonchalant shrug. "I hope I didn't sound like I was showing off or anything. See, my father's a professional actor. He's worked with various theaters in the D.C. area over the years, including the Folger. I guess I first got interested in drama because of him. He lives and breathes it. When I was in about sixth grade, I auditioned for my first kid's role, and ever since then I've been doing that sort of thing now and then, mostly at the Folger and the Arena Stage. But then I started to grow up" — Buford wiggled his eyebrows comically and Lily giggled — "and for the last few years I've been doing less of it. A lot of adult actors can look young enough to play teenagers, so auditions are much more competitive. But last semester I was asked to play a tiny part in *Macbeth*. My dad was in the production also, and I played the part of his son, which made it a lot of fun."

Lily was altogether dazzled by this speech. As she stared at Buford, something dawned on her through her haze. "*That's* why I thought I'd seen you before!" she exclaimed, hitting the palm of her hand against her forehead. "I must have seen you before, in plays in D.C." Lily frowned, wanting to get every detail straight. "But I can't figure out why I didn't remember your name when I first heard it. I don't usually forget an actor or a role, either!"

Buford grinned wryly. "And nobody could forget the name Buford Wodjovodski, right?" Lily nodded, swallowing a giggle as her conversation with Frankie and Stacy before the auditions sprang to mind. "In the past I've used the stage name Ford Miller," he explained. "Ford is for Buford, and Miller is my mom's maiden name. Pretty clever, huh? When I was a kid I was totally embarrassed about having a name no one could spell, much less pronounce. I mean, admit it, Buford Wodjovodski is the world's nerdiest name!" Lily couldn't contradict him, and Buford just laughed. "It's funny, though," he added. "Now that I'm older I'm actually starting to like my name a little. It's unique, to say the least. And it's mine." He winked. "So maybe next time out I'll use Buford Wodjovodski. What do you think?"

"Go for it!" Lily encouraged. "And anyway, *this* time out you're using it — in *Twelfth Night*. 'Buford Wodjovodski' in neon lights at the Kennedy High Little Theater!"

"They got lights here?" he asked, pretending to be surprised.

"Hey, this is the big time!" Lily and Buford both burst out laughing.

Lily had been so absorbed by her conversation with Buford that she hadn't felt the minutes flying by. They were no longer alone in the lobby of the Little Theater. Other students who'd landed roles in *Twelfth Night* were drifting in. She examined her watch. Yep, it was time for the first rehearsal. As if to confirm Lily's observation,

Mrs. Weiss poked her head between the double doors that opened into the main part of the theater and gave a loud whistle.

Lily and Buford jumped to their feet and followed the last of the loitering students inside. Mrs. Weiss handed them each a copy of the script, and they joined the others onstage. People were sitting in a circle on the dusty floor, legs crossed Indian-style. In addition to the basic uniform of sweat-shirt and jeans, everyone wore an identical first-rehearsal expression: excited, serious, nervous, proud.

Lily stepped up onto the stage. Her toes were tingling, which wasn't strange considering the circumstances, but she knew her enthusiasm wasn't entirely due to the fact that she'd been cast as Viola. First of all, she was smiling so hard her mouth ached. All the other kids looked funereal in comparison. Secondly, her feet hardly seemed to touch the ground as she crossed the stage. She had a distinctly peculiar sensation, as if her body were doing one thing while her mind was off somewhere else. And that place had nothing to do with Viola, *Twelfth Night*, or even old Will Shakespeare himself. As she sat down next to Buford in the circle, Lily realized that she was aware of his presence to the exclusion of anything else. If she didn't make space in her mind for the rest of the world, she was going to have a hard time with the read-through.

Lily concentrated on pushing Buford out of her thoughts. But the moment she succeeded, Jonathan pushed his way in. Surprised, Lily unintentionally dropped her script. The pages fluttered like autumn leaves as it fell to the ground. She bent forward to retrieve the script, glad that her falling hair hid her flustered expression from Buford.

Jonathan. Lily pictured her boyfriend's face and suddenly found herself coming back to earth with a thud. I broke my rule, she thought dismally. Not only did I talk to Buford, but I *liked* talking to Buford. I like *Buford*! She snuck a peek at him out of the corner of her eye. He was studying his script, making notes in the margin, and also listening to Mrs. Weiss, who was explaining her goals for this initial rehearsal. Lily looked down at her own script and bit her lip, unsure of how far she'd actually strayed. Maybe she'd broken her own rule, but she hadn't really betrayed Jonathan, had she? He couldn't expect her to go through life never exchanging a single word with an unattached male, especially when she'd be working with Buford and these other guys every day after school for the next month and a half!

No, talking to Buford didn't constitute betrayal. But Lily knew that just plain talking could lead to a lot of things. Look at her relationship with Jonathan. Look at any relationship. A conversation at a football game, in the hall between classes, in the cafeteria, before a play rehearsal — that's how romance started. The thing to do was to set a new rule for herself, one she could really keep.

Okay. Lily clenched her teeth, determined. She could talk to Buford until she was blue in the face if she wanted to, as long as their talks didn't get to be . . . serious. If she found herself liking him too much, she had to pull back. And certainly accepting a date would be out of the question. There, that was a good rule. It was fair to Jonathan and fair to herself.

Lily stole another glance at Buford. Under the soft stage lights, he looked even more handsome than he had in the lobby a few minutes ago. Despite her love for Jonathan and her sincere desire to make their relationship work, she couldn't stop a small but insistent doubt from curling itself up in a cold ball in her stomach. Making rules and keeping promises — why did it have to be so hard?

Chapter
7

"Where is everybody, anyway?" asked Stacy. The warm breeze blew her curly hair across her face as she scanned the quad.

Lily raised one eyebrow and looked at Frankie, then back at Stacy. "What are *we*, chopped liver?" she wondered, pretending to be offended.

"What I meant was, where is everybody *else*?" Stacy amended with a grin.

Frankie ticked the names off on her fingers. "Greg has a student council meeting, and Daniel is probably — make that definitely — grinding away at the newspaper office. I bumped into Roxanne on my way out, and she said she was going to work on the yearbook during lunch. Then I bumped into Vince, who as usual these days looked preoccupied and depressed. I don't think he even saw me. And Josh is on the air." Frankie pointed out into space, as if Josh as well as his radio show were present in the atmosphere. "I don't know about Zack, though. He's your department, Stacy. Wasn't he going to meet us out here?"

Stacy, now lying on top of her denim jacket with her still-tanned face turned toward the sun, nodded with a slight grimace. "He's supposed to meet us," she confirmed. "I saw him with my own eyes in the cafeteria while I was buying my sandwich. He was trying to make his way to the door to catch up with me, but he was blocked by adoring female football fans every step of the way." Stacy had to giggle as she recalled the sight. "He doesn't have any trouble getting past the opposing team's defense, but when it comes to a mob like that, forget it!"

"Fame is tough," Lily observed as she tipped her own face skyward. "But I get the feeling Zack can handle it."

"Yeah, he probably can," Stacy agreed lightly. She didn't add the question she asked herself: But *how* will he handle it? By shrugging it off, making a joke out of it? Or by totally getting involved in it — and involved with the dozens of girls who were so eager to remind him how great he was? Stacy didn't say anything about her doubts, not wanting to believe that they could have any foundation in reality. She'd declared her absolute trust in Zachary to her friends. They'd taken her word for it, and now she found herself wanting to believe it as much as they did.

"After tonight, though, Zack's going to have an even harder time making his way through the hallways and the cafeteria," predicted Frankie. She pulled an apple out of her lunch bag and twisted off the stem. "It's going to be another big victory!"

Stacy sat up again, brushing a few blades of dry grass off the sleeves of her red polo shirt. Her eyes sparkled. "Wheaton High doesn't have a chance. The Kennedy football team is undefeated, and they're going to stay that way!"

Lily smiled at Stacy's cheerleader's enthusiasm. "Go, team, go!" shouted Lily, waving imaginary pom-poms. Stacy gave her a good-natured shove. Laughing, Lily shoved back.

Frankie distracted them. "Speak of the devil," she said, "here comes Zack."

Stacy and Lily stopped clowning and looked along with Frankie in the direction of the south wing. The heavy door had just swung closed behind Zachary, who was now crossing the quad heading in their direction. He walked with the long, easy strides of an athlete, his varsity jacket slung carelessly over one shoulder and a typically open, friendly smile on his face. Even from this distance as Zack looked her way, Stacy could see the warm, eager look in his eyes. Inside she knew that it was meant exclusively for her, all those cute girls in the cafeteria notwithstanding. Her heart melted.

Before Zachary made it halfway across the lawn, however, he was intercepted by a girl in a frilly white blouse and a billowing, lace-edged prairie skirt. Stacy's eyes narrowed. It was Charlotte. Without meaning to, Stacy glanced sharply at Lily and Frankie, both of whom looked at her at the same time. The faces of all three girls registered the same uncertain, apprehensive expression.

Since their conversation with Jana Lacey at the sub shop, none of them had known quite what to think about Char. It took an effort not to view their friend differently than they had before. It took a *real* effort for Stacy, and as she watched Charlotte treat Zachary to her brightest smile, putting a hand on his arm and leaning toward him flirtatiously as she did so, Stacy's heart curled up in a tight ball. It took too much of an effort to think fairly about Charlotte. Sure, Char was known for her warm, southern manner, for her way of greeting everybody as if they were a long-lost sister or brother. But even so, Stacy couldn't help growing suspicious, especially as she watched Zack smile back at Charlotte with, if it were possible, even more pleasure than Char herself had exhibited.

Stacy bit her lip. All of a sudden she felt as if she'd been spun back in time to the beginning of the summer, when she first fell for Zack. All her former insecurities — Does he like me? Does he even know I exist? — came bouncing back to her like a tennis ball thrown against a brick wall. Stacy kept her face turned slightly away from Frankie and Lily, not wanting them to see how much this scene bothered her. It just wasn't like Zack to be *that* exuberant and outgoing, even with a good friend. Was his Super Bowl smile a special order for Charlotte? Or was he just warmed up from smiling at all those girls in the cafeteria? Stacy wasn't sure which idea made her more nervous.

Stacy didn't have a chance to make up her mind before Zack and Charlotte finished smiling at each other and joined the three girls where they were sitting on the grass beneath the gang's favorite cherry tree.

"Well, hello, ladies!" Charlotte couldn't have seemed happier to see them.

Stacy did her best to appear unperturbed. "Hi, Char, have a seat," she invited. Despite her efforts, she could tell she didn't sound very sincere.

Lily made up for Stacy's lack of enthusiasm by adding, "Hi, Charlotte! It's nice to see you! Isn't the weather great? I love your blouse," in her brightest, most bubbly voice.

Meanwhile, Zachary had dropped to the ground next to Stacy. Stacy half held her breath, secretly afraid. Would he kiss her hello? Or when he looked at her, would that special something be missing from his eyes? Before Zack could even turn to Stacy, however, his attention was diverted by Charlotte, who'd carefully seated herself on his other side. With her full skirt spread out in a wide circle around her she looked like Scarlett O'Hara at the Twelve Oaks barbecue.

Charlotte had her hand on Zachary's arm again in the same flirty, possessive way. "Zack, I hope you haven't forgotten that you promised to help me move chairs for the dance next Friday," she cooed. "I'm just reminding you because I know it's probably the furthest thing from your mind. All you're thinking about these days is football, football, football, am I right?"

Zachary shrugged but he couldn't help looking

86

pleased as Char went on to praise his latest achievements as quarterback and predict another big win in the game that evening.

Stacy suddenly wished she hadn't just eaten that enormous tuna hero; she felt a little nauseated. Charlotte wasn't really saying anything very different from what Stacy, Frankie, and Lily had been saying among themselves a few minutes earlier. Zack *had* been playing fantastically well, and Kennedy probably *would* clobber the visiting team in tonight's game. It was the way she said it that bothered Stacy. Charlotte didn't just talk with her voice — she fluttered her eyelashes, pursed her lips, and tossed her hair in a way that had never bothered Stacy before, but which right at this minute was just about driving her crazy. And if Char didn't stop squeezing Zack's arm *fast*, Stacy was sure she'd scream.

Before Stacy could scream or do anything else, Lily broke into Charlotte's rapturous monologue. "Getting back to the dance, Char," Lily began, darting a meaningful glance at Frankie and Stacy, "I'm free during lunch periods. I could help move chairs, too, if you want."

Frankie picked up on Lily's lead. "Me, too," she offered eagerly. "Count me in."

Stacy had to restrain herself from leaping up to give her two friends a hug. Clearly their thoughts were running along the same lines as hers. With every passing minute, the story Jana had told them about Charlotte seemed more and more on target. And knowing that Stacy herself would be tied up with the spirit rally, Frankie and Lily were cleverly plotting to be present at the chair-moving session to foil any designs Char might have on Zachary.

But Stacy's relief and gratitude were short-lived. Instead of accepting Lily and Frankie's offer, Charlotte waved them off with a delicate, well-manicured hand. "Thanks a lot for volunteering, you two," she said lightly. "But I really can't use you. The chairs are *very* heavy — moving them will be *men's* work." Char paused to give Zack's left bicep an illustrative squeeze. Zack grinned proudly, and Stacy clenched her teeth. "So, I'll only need guys!" Charlotte concluded, dimpling. "If you're interested in helping out, though, you could get involved with decorating the theater later that afternoon. I'll pass your names along to Marla Hughes, who's my decorations chair. Okay?"

Lily had to nod to keep from exploding. Moving chairs — *men's* work? What a line! Char could have at least covered herself by saying she had plenty of volunteers.

Charlotte rose gracefully to her feet and like a true gentleman, Zack handed Char her books. "I've got to run," she announced in a cheerful tone. "While it's on my mind, I think I'll just hunt up Greg and Josh and remind *them* about helping with the chairs! See y'all later!"

With a flounce of her ruffly skirt, Charlotte turned to head back across the quad toward the school building. The three girls watched her go in stunned silence. Zack, oblivious to any tension in the air, folded his hands behind his head and leaned back against the bench, placidly enjoying the sunshine.

Stacy wedged her hands into the front pockets of her khakis, thinking hard. There was no longer any doubt about it in her opinion. Jana Lacey had been all too accurate in her depiction of Char as a ruthless flirt and boyfriend-stealer. And she had been one all along; her new friends had just been blinded by her southern-style sweetness. But Stacy's eyes were open now. Here was Charlotte making a play for Zack, and probably Greg and Josh, too, right in front of two out of the three boys' girlfriends! It was unbelievable! But Stacy wasn't about to leave the field to Charlotte undefended. If Char wanted Zack, she'd have to fight for him and fight hard.

The first thing to do, clearly, was to prevent Zack from helping Charlotte get ready for the dance by moving those stupid chairs. Stacy plucked a handful of grass and without thinking began shredding the slim blades as she faced her boyfriend. "Zack, I know you promised to take the seats out of the theater with Char," she said. Her long-lashed eyes were determined. "But I really wish you'd come to my spirit rally that lunch period instead."

Zack opened his eyes lazily, putting a hand to his forehead to block out the bright sun. "Well, I will be at your rally, for the first few minutes, anyway," he reminded her. It was a spirit rally tradition for the football team to jog around the field house during the cheerleaders' first routine. "I was going to help Char in the Little Theater afterward."

"But I'd really like you to stay for the whole rally," Stacy insisted, her expression serious.

Zachary tipped his head to one side, puzzled. "How come?" he wondered.

"Well . . ." Stacy blushed slightly. She didn't want Zack to guess the real reason. "I think it's important for all the football players to hang around. It looks better, from the point of view of school spirit. And . . . and I'd just like you to be there for me. It would mean a lot. I mean, you're the reason I'm cheering, anyhow." That much was certainly true, Stacy thought to herself. "Besides, Charlotte will have plenty of other people to help her," she concluded logically. "I'm sure she can spare you."

Zachary seemed touched by Stacy's request. "Okay. If that's the way you feel, I'll stick around at the rally." He leaned forward to brush a strand of hair off Stacy's cheek. His lingering touch, gentle and affectionate, caused her face to grow warm.

"Thanks, Zack," Stacy said softly.

"Hey, what are boyfriends for?" Zachary smiled, his bright blue eyes cheerful and innocent. A few seconds later he squinted. "Is that Bill Markowitz over there?" When Stacy confirmed that it was, Zack jumped to his feet. "Coach wanted me to tell him to show up for the pregame warm-up a little early," he explained. "Bill's the second-string quarterback and it looks like he's going to have a chance to play the fourth quarter tonight. That is, if we get off to a fast start and score a few touchdowns early — which I'm planning on. Be right back!"

Zachary hurried off to talk to Bill. The minute he was out of earshot, Stacy, Lily, and Frankie all started to talk at once. "Did you see the way she didn't take her eyes or her hands off Zack the entire time she was talking to him?"

"Could you believe it when she said she didn't need any girls to help her with the chairs? I *bet* she doesn't need any girls!"

"I just never would have thought it of someone who seems as nice as Charlotte!"

All three shook their heads dismally. "I never would have thought it," Frankie repeated, looking as if she still didn't want to believe the worst.

"Well, think it," Lily said bluntly. "It's the truth. As a rule I wouldn't trust Jana Lacey farther than I could throw her, but this time it really looks like she knows what she's talking about. If we didn't just see a boyfriend-stealer in action, I don't know what we saw!" Lily turned quickly to Stacy, her dark eyes softening with concern. "Not that she's stolen him yet," she corrected herself. "But she's trying."

"What am I going to do?" Stacy asked anxiously.

"What are *we* going to do?" Frankie's expression was just as worried. "Josh is almost as much of a target as Zack. I mean, Charlotte's enlisted him to help move chairs, too!"

"Well, we shouldn't panic," Lily assured her friends. She crossed her thin arms in a determined manner. "After all, there's only one of her and there's three of us. And we have an advantage — we're onto her game. We just have to do everything we can to protect the guys in our circle of friends from her."

"I'll talk Josh out of helping with the chairs somehow," Frankie said, inspired.

Stacy brightened. "And I'll talk to Greg, since Katie isn't here to do it herself."

"And we should all keep our eyes on Charlotte," Lily concluded. "I'm sure the chair scheme isn't the only one she has up her sleeve — no *wonder* she's friends with Roxanne!"

When the bell rang, signaling the end of lunch, Stacy put on her jacket and collected her books. Lily and Frankie were in a hurry because they had to stop at their lockers before their next classes, but Stacy took her time, pulling a comb through her windblown hair as she waited for Zachary to rejoin her. As they strolled across the grass together a few minutes later, she snuck a glance at him out of the corner of her eye. She guessed he didn't look any different than usual — maybe a little more buoyant and confident, but that was because of the whole football star thing. It didn't mean he'd been taken in by Charlotte's wiles. He wasn't caught in her web yet.

As they neared the door, Zack took Stacy's hand and gave it a light squeeze. She squeezed it back, firmly. And I'm not letting go, she said silently. Y'all hear that, Charlotte DeVries?

Chapter
8

Sara Gates pushed up the long sleeves of her pink-and-white-striped rugby shirt and tapped one foot nervously. From where she stood, leaning against the wall next to the water fountain outside the newspaper office, she had a wide-open view of the herds of students passing by, all rushing down the corridor in the direction of the cafeteria and lunch. Every second student held in his or her hand a copy of the *The Red and the Gold*, which had hit campus just that morning. Some people had turned to the back of the paper and the full-page spread detailing the Kennedy High football team's undefeated season. The coverage included photos from Friday night's Cardinal victory, which Daniel had developed and rushed to the printer's on Saturday, just two days before the paper was due to come out. Other students scanned the front page and the index to the school, community, and national news articles contained inside. Were any of them reading the movie reviews? Sara wondered, feeling both hopeful and anxious. It was hard to tell.

Sara stepped up the pace of her foot-tapping as she pictured page seven of *The Red and the Gold*, where her two reviews were positioned side by side. They looked great, and she'd already surreptitiously stashed a dozen or so copies of the paper in her locker. Her father might want to see one — if he had a spare minute, and she'd send a copy to both sets of grandparents, too. Then she needed one for her scrapbook, and one for the professional portfolio she was going to begin building, and so on. Yes, Sara thought, her articles *looked* nice. But were they actually any good? In the past she'd never had any doubts about her basic writing ability. As for her knowledge of and enthusiasm for movies — old, new, foreign, you name it, she could cover them all. But since the start of the school year, working with Daniel in the pressure cooker he'd created out of the tame old newspaper room, Sara wasn't so sure. Not only was she beginning to wonder whether she had any journalistic talent worth speaking of, but she was also starting to wonder if she was going to be able to hack *The Red and the Gold* and its demanding editor-in-chief. So far, working on the newspaper every day during lunch periods and after school had left her physically and emotionally drained. And these were only the first few issues of the school year!

"Congratulations! Your movie reviews are absolutely awesome!"

Sara jumped a couple of feet off the ground.

She had been so busy trying to read the minds of the kids walking by — were they reading her articles, and if so, what did they think of them? — that she didn't notice her boyfriend, Torrey Easton, until he was right behind her.

Torrey gently grasped Sara's shoulders and swung her around to face him. "Congratulations!" he repeated, reaching into the back pocket of his jeans to pull out a somewhat wrinkled copy of *The Red and the Gold*. His handsome face creased in a proud smile. "Your stuff is great. I was really impressed."

Sara raised her blonde eyebrows, still uncertain. Torrey's praise warmed her right down to the toes of her Tretorns, but maybe as her boyfriend he was biased. It was even possible he was just being polite. He'd know she expected him to say *something*. "You really liked my reviews?" Sara asked, wrinkling her freckled nose in disbelief. "Did you read them carefully? I mean, with a critical eye? Here," Sara took the paper from Torrey and opened it to the arts section. "Read them again. Pretend you don't know who wrote them."

"I've read them both *five* times. Me — Torrey Easton! It's the most I've read in a whole year!" He snatched the newspaper out of Sara's hands and tossed it in the air. The pages fluttered down around them like huge confetti. "They're concise and insightful and authoritative and creative. . . ." Torrey rattled off the adjectives with a goofy grin. Then he seemed to look at Sara, really look at her, for the first time since they'd started talking. "Hey, Sara," he said, lowering his voice and touching one finger to her flushed cheek. "What's the matter? Don't *you* think your reviews are good?"

Torrey's tenderness caused Sara's throat to tighten. She bit back the threatening tears, determined not to make a scene. "No . . . yes . . . oh, I don't know!" she exclaimed, her voice cracking slightly. "I guess I thought they were good when I first wrote them. But then when Daniel made me rewrite and rewrite and rewrite them. . . ." She nodded rhythmically as she spoke to indicate a never-ending process. "It seemed like every time I revised one of the reviews, Daniel liked it even less than the last version. To tell you the truth, I'm surprised he even printed either of these. Basically, he thinks I'm an illiterate dope. I'm pretty sure he's sorry he asked me to be on his staff. But I don't know — I might just beat him to the punch by quitting before he can fire me!"

Sara hadn't meant to spill all this out to Torrey, but once she started talking, the intensity of her feelings on the subject pushed her on. Now she sniffled, still making a heroic effort not to cry. Torrey didn't respond to her outburst right away. Instead, he put one arm firmly around her shoulders and walked her toward the nearest stairwell. After steering her through the door, Torrey pulled Sara down next to him as he took a seat on the top step. The stairwell was empty; the between-classes traffic had abated. Torrey's deep voice echoed strangely around the gray, cement-and-iron walls. First he asked softly, "Are you okay, Sar?" When she nodded, wiping at her eyes with the back of her hand, he continued in a brisker tone. "I can't

96

believe you're thinking about dropping the newspaper. I knew Daniel was a tough guy, but I didn't know he was that bad!"

Sara shrugged her slender shoulders, pulling her knees up to wrap her arms around them. "But like I said, he has a point. He's not just tough for the sake of being tough." Her voice faltered. "My writing isn't up to his standards, that's all there is to it."

Torrey frowned, his dark eyebrows meeting in an angry knot over the bridge of his nose. "That's garbage and you know it. You're an excellent writer — the reviews in this week's issue are evidence of that."

"But — "

"Nope. No buts." Torrey tipped his head to one side. A shock of dark hair fell in front of his puzzled eyes. "Hey, this doesn't sound like the Sara Gates I know and love. It doesn't sound like the girl I met at the Video Stop in the mall this summer, the one who talked me into giving myself a chance, working for what I wanted." Torrey's voice had grown low and husky. "That girl wouldn't let someone like Daniel Tackett get her down."

Slowly, Sara turned her gray-blue eyes to Torrey. Her discouraged expression faded as she met his caring, challenging gaze. Torrey's words had taken her right back to the hot summer afternoon when he had stopped by the Video Stop, where she was working. They recognized each other, but had never spoken before. All Sara knew about Torrey Easton was what was said about him at school: that he was practically a delinquent, a bad-attitude kid who'd transferred from Stevenson High along with his older sister, Roxanne. But unlike the glamorous, ambitious Rox, Torrey had made no attempt to fit in at Kennedy. When Torrey hung out with anybody — he was pretty much a loner — it was with the kind of kids who cut school more than they attended. That afternoon in the video store, Sara had recommended that Torrey rent the movie *Breaking Away*. From that moment on, they'd played an important part in each other's lives. Sara had been unhappy, too. Her parents were divorced like Torrey's, but while Torrey and Roxanne lived with an indifferent mother, Sara lived with a workaholic — and alcoholic — father. With Torrey, Sara had discovered the love and support she'd never experienced at home, and she had done the same for him.

Now she dropped her eyes, ashamed. "I know I probably sound like I'm wimping out," she admitted, her voice small. "It's just hard not to. Daniel has this way of making me feel about this big." Sara held up one hand, indicating a tiny amount with her thumb and index finger. "You know exactly what he's like," she said, referring to the biking article Torrey had submitted to *The Red and the Gold*. Daniel had completely dismissed it as the work of an illiterate.

Torrey shook his head. "You're all wrong. Inside, you're the biggest, strongest person I know. You shouldn't let Daniel talk you into forgetting that." Torrey had been speaking in a firm, encouraging tone, but now, for just a moment, an edge of bitterness crept in. "Why do we always let other people put us down and then react by doing things that only hurt ourselves? Sara, you wanted more than anything in the world to be on this newspaper, and you deserve the position. You shouldn't give it up just because Daniel Tackett is acting like a dictator. Why don't you just march into that office and tell him that he's treating you unfairly? Stand up for yourself!"

Suddenly Sara didn't feel like crying anymore. Torrey was right. She'd let Daniel's intimidating tactics trample all over her faith in her writing and her confidence in herself. She looked up, pushing her strawberry blonde hair back from her tear-streaked face. Torrey was watching her, his dark eyes expectant and concerned. A warmth started in Sara's heart and spread slowly but surely thought her entire body. She was so lucky to have Torrey — he was the truest friend she'd ever known. She smiled broadly at him. "Thanks for the pep talk," she said with a hiccup. "I didn't know how much I needed one."

Torrey leaned toward Sara, wrapping his arms tightly around her. "You know where to come whenever you want to talk to somebody who thinks you're the greatest thing around," he whispered into her hair.

Sara pulled back so she could give him a quick, soft kiss. Then she slipped from his arms and jumped to her feet. Torrey stood up as well. "I think I'm going to take your advice — right this minute," she announced, looking determined. "I'm going to tell Daniel how I feel. I'll tell him he'd better change his ways fast, or he's going to lose a darn good movie reviewer!"

"Atta girl!" Torrey cheered, grabbing her around the waist and twirling her in circles until they were both dizzy and giggling. When he set her down, Sara was grinning from ear to ear. She was still smiling as she headed purposefully down the hall in the direction of the newspaper office, turning to wave at Torrey as he headed into the cafeteria. But her momentum had faded slightly by the time she reached the door. She stood with her hand poised just above the knob, wondering what had happened to all the nerve she'd mustered up a minute before. Did she really want to confront her editor-in-chief? Sara pictured Daniel's closed, stern face and wilted a little bit inside. Then she pictured Torrey, smiling at her with belief and love. She turned the knob and pushed the door open.

As usual, Daniel was sitting at his desk with his head bent over his work. Other than him, the cluttered office was empty. It looked to Sara as if the rest of the staff was taking a much-deserved day off. Would Daniel actually have authorized such a thing? It didn't seem likely. Sara guessed the other kids had probably given in to the same urge to play hooky that she had.

Sara approached Daniel, stepping as quietly as she could. When he swiveled his chair around to face her after she said a tentative hello, she realized she didn't have the vaguest idea how to begin. "Hi, Sara," he responded in his typically gruff manner.

"Um, Daniel." Sara swallowed twice. Her toes curled up inside her sneakers and for the life of her she didn't think she'd be able to utter another word. Then she saw her opening. A copy of *The Red and the Gold* was lying open on top of Daniel's desk, and it was actually turned to page seven, the arts section. "Uh, I was wondering . . ." Sara nodded at the newspaper. "Is there anything wrong . . . has there been anything wrong, I mean *really* wrong, with my movie reviews?"

Daniel's dark eyebrows shot up. His cool, green eyes registered his surprise. "Anything wrong?" he repeated somewhat blankly as he tipped back in his chair and swung his feet casually. "No, not at all. On the contrary, your reviews are great, definitely the high point of the arts section so far."

Sara couldn't believe her ears. Naturally she had been expecting the worst, but Daniel couldn't have said anything that more completely contradicted all of his prior words and actions. What kind of games did Daniel think he could play with her? An angry, awkward flush stole across her face. "If you're pleased with my reviews, then how come you always act as if they're totally off track?" The firm sound of her own voice gave Sara additional courage, and she continued even more emphatically. "All I ever hear is how sloppy and inadequate my writing is, even though I spend hours and hours working over each paragraph. You know, it wouldn't hurt for you to be nice to your staff now and then! Everybody would probably be a lot happier sacrificing all their spare time to *The Red and the Gold* if they got a little appreciation in return."

Daniel dropped his chair back to the ground with a clatter and stared at Sara, speechless. She hesitated for a moment and then decided she wouldn't wait for him to answer. She'd given him something to think about, and right now all she wanted to do was escape, fast. She spun around, her hair flying, and bolted for the door, jerking it closed behind her with a bang. Once in the hall, her knees buckled slightly. She'd done it! She'd actually stood up to Daniel Tackett. She'd stood up for herself and for all the other kids on the staff who'd been getting the same shabby treatment. And it hadn't even been that hard. She should have given him a piece of her mind weeks ago.

Sara lifted her chin proudly. Maybe Daniel would still fire her, but she didn't care. She was in the right, and she'd preserved her dignity. Sara hurried down the hall toward the cafeteria. She couldn't wait to tell Torrey.

The newspaper office still echoed from the slammed door as Daniel rotated slowly back around in his chair to face his desk again. He took a deep breath and then let it out with a long, dissatisfied sigh. Daniel hated to admit it, but Sara's words had cut right through him. As she spoke, he'd seen for the first time since school had started how bitterly he'd been behaving. He *had* been giving her a hard time about her reviews when she deserved just the opposite. She was a better writer than practically anybody else on the paper, with the exception of himself, of course.

Daniel picked up a pencil and fidgeted with it. He closed his eyes, recalling his past conversations with Sara. They weren't conversations, really. On every single occasion he'd criticized her work.

And not only had he criticized her, he'd snapped and scowled and been generally as cold and sour as a refrigerator full of lemons. And as Sara herself had pointed out, she wasn't the only one Daniel had treated roughly. Nobody on the staff had been exempted from his tyrannical methods and attitudes.

Snap. Daniel looked down, surprised to see that he'd broken the pencil in two. With an irritated shake of his head, he threw the splintered pieces against the wall. He knew he owed Sara and the others an apology. He wasn't the only person who'd slaved to make the early issues of *The Red and the Gold* a success — they'd all done the same, and the paper wouldn't be as good as it was without their efforts. Daniel reached for the issue of *The Red and the Gold* lying open on his desk and closed it. He studied the front page, admiring the headlines. Then he opened to the second page, to the masthead column. There he was, right at the top. He flipped through the entire paper and when he reached the end, a powerful feeling of accomplishment coursed through him. It was a good paper, a very good paper. It was far better than anything he'd put together while he was editor of the *Stevenson Sentinel*. He owed Sara and the rest of the staff more than an apology. He owed them his most sincere thanks.

Daniel pushed the paper aside and bent forward with his head on his arms. The clean, vaguely chemical smell of newsprint tickled his nose, but he wasn't thinking of Sara or *The Red and the Gold* anymore. He was thinking about the reason he'd been so short-tempered with everyone around him for the past few weeks. Unfortunately, it was a reason he didn't think was going to go away. The reason was Lin, and Daniel was pretty sure he'd never see her again. The problem and his unhappiness were here to stay.

Chapter 9

Lily made her way slowly along the sidewalk toward the Little Theater, kicking at the piles of fallen leaves as she went. The sharp wind whipped her hair across her face and pushed her forward — she felt almost as if she could let herself fall backward and the air would support her. It was a gorgeous afternoon, too nice to spend in the musty, dusty theater. But Mrs. Weiss had asked the entire *Twelfth Night* cast to meet her a little early in the costume storage room before the day's rehearsal, and Lily knew she shouldn't dawdle, as much as she was tempted.

The breeze blew Lily up to the door of the theater and right inside. She brushed a few stray leaves from her bulky sweater as she hurried through the lobby and into the auditorium. There was no one around. Lily figured the cast must already be assembling in the costume room. As she hopped onto the stage, pushed through the moth-eaten green velvet curtain, and wove her way around the junk backstage to end up in front of a door that was badly in need of paint marked "Costumes," she suddenly had an odd feeling of *déjà vu*. She froze for a second, trying to place the sensation, but just as she was about to put her finger on it, it faded away. Lily shook her head and opened the door.

The costume room had always seemed enormous, dark, and drafty to Lily, but with the entire cast lounging around, it had become almost cozy and warm. Mrs. Weiss was already talking, so Lily sat down as inconspicuously as she could on top of a somewhat shabby and unsturdy box marked "Greek and Roman sandals."

Mrs. Weiss paused in her remarks to run a hand through her short, wavy auburn hair. "So, after a lot of thinking I've decided on a modern-dress production." She smiled at the cast's exclamations. "Don't you think that will add to the fun?" There were nods of assent all around. "Rehearsals have been going very well, even better than I'd expected, and I think we've reached the point where we should begin practicing in at least partial costume," Mrs. Weiss continued. "And since you all know your characters better than anyone else does, I'd like you each to choose your own costumes. That's why we're here right now. Feel free to pick out anything that seems appropriate, I have faith in your good judgment. Just meet me back onstage in, say . . . twenty minutes, dressed and ready to go!"

Lily's face was practically splitting wide open from her smile. Modern dress! she thought happily. Choose our own costumes! That was just the sort of production Lily enjoyed most. Mrs. Weiss was right — it would be more fun, and it allowed each actor and actress to contribute that much more to the individual interpretation of his or her character. Lily approved entirely.

The moment Mrs. Weiss finished giving instructions, the cast flew into motion, rifling through the hanging costumes and the boxes of shirts and pants, trying on hats, scarves, and other colorful accessories, and generally making a racket. Lily jumped up to join in the action, not wanting to miss out on the best costume pieces. The first carton she plunged into yielded a wonderful pair of baggy pants, with some green-and-orange-striped suspenders still attached. She held them up with satisfaction. They were very Charlie Chaplinish — exactly what she had in mind for Viola, who was disguised as a boy for most of the play. Lily felt her costume, therefore, should *look* like a costume.

Lily was just about to slip the trousers on over her slim-fitting black leggings when a deep, musical voice called her name. Her heart, which had been racing with general theater-related excitement, now broke into a full-fledged gallop. Lily straightened up and turned cautiously to face Buford.

Ever since the first rehearsal, Lily had been playing it safe where Buford was concerned. She arrived for practice right on time and left the moment Mrs. Weiss dismissed her, never putting herself in a position where she'd be just hanging around with time to chat casually with Buford, or anyone else in the cast for that matter. Lily was having fun participating in *Twelfth Night* — it would be impossible not to — but her attitude was strictly business. She knew that if she let herself go, really let herself get carried away by the carefree, electric spirit when she was working on a play, she'd be lost. Or rather, her relationship with Jonathan would be lost. She had to look upon Buford as a colleague and nothing more. It was essential that she preserve a friendly but cool distance between them.

But it was hard, especially since Buford had been making it clear to her ever since that first day that he would like to get to know her better. And Lily had a feeling that Buford was the kind of guy who sooner or later got what he wanted. Now he was standing in front of her wearing a cranberry-and-black brocade smoking jacket, a jauntily knotted ascot, and a pair of funny old-fashioned. Ben Franklin-style eyeglasses. Lily tried to be stern with herself, but she simply couldn't help laughing.

"Is this Malvolio or what?" Buford asked, holding his hands out, palms up, for emphasis. He grinned and wiggled his eyebrows.

Lily nodded, still laughing. "It's perfect!" she agreed. Then her smile became mischievous. "Except for the glasses. . . . I think Malvolio would go more for dark, Italian sunglasses. You know, the European look. Those, however, would be great for Viola — just the finishing touch I was looking for." Lily hopped forward and stood on her tiptoes to pluck the eyelasses right off Buford's straight, slender nose.

Buford took a swipe at her hand but missed. "Oh, no you don't!" he declared. His voice boomed authoritatively, but his eyes were twinkling. "I discovered them. And the way *I* read ol' Mal, they're his style all right!" Lily had popped the glasses onto her own nose and they wobbled slightly, oversized. "See, they don't even fit you," Buford pointed out reasonably. "Unhand them, madam."

Lily stepped away from Buford, her eyes teasing. "If you want them, come and get them!"

A moment later, Buford was chasing Lily around a rack of rustling taffeta dresses. She did a good job of evading him until she tripped over an inconveniently placed pearl-handled walking stick and fell halfway into a huge box of corsets and petticoats. Buford bent over Lily, his hands placed firmly on the rims of the carton on either side of her. "The glasses or your virtue," he proposed in a western-movie drawl.

Lily sighed with exaggerated resignation, pretending to be cornered. Then she reached up suddenly and tickled Buford, squirming out of the box as she did so, the glasses still perched triumphantly on her nose. She didn't get far. Buford grabbed her by one foot and they both collapsed, laughing, into a heap of old costumes.

"Say 'uncle,' " Buford demanded, still gripping Lily's left ankle.

"Uncle, uncle!" she exclaimed between giggles. "Here are your dumb glasses!" Buford leaned closer to Lily so that she could repentently place them back on the nose of their rightful owner. His face was only inches away from hers and she could smell the crisp, fall scent that clung to his clothes. All of a sudden Lily froze, her hands still holding the eyeglasses. How had she let herself get so open and playful with Buford Wodjovodski? Someone looking at them from the outside would certainly think that Lily was more than a little interested in Buford. She'd broken the rule she'd made for herself — and how. Not only that, but there was something strangely familiar about this scene. The sensation of *déjà vu* rushed back over Lily, and this time she knew exactly why she felt as if she'd been in this situation before — because she *had* been. She had, except that she'd been in it with Jonathan, not Buford. She'd first met Jonathan right here, in the costume storage room. It was the previous spring and she'd been hunting for some costume accessories to wear for her mime role in *The Fantasticks*. She and Jonathan hadn't known one another, and the conversation had begun with Jonathan rather sourly accusing Lily of attempting to make off with his precious fedora. She'd playfully fought him for it, and soon they were both laughing uproariously. The attraction had been immediate for both of them.

And now here she was, playing in the costume room with Buford. The guilt was overpowering. Lily dropped her gaze from Buford's and simply handed him the glasses. She shifted slightly, preparing to stand up, collect the costume pieces she'd selected, and make a speedy getaway. Unfortunately, she couldn't extricate herself from the tangle of costumes unless Buford moved first, and he didn't look like he was going anywhere. If possible, the guilt Lily was feeling just about doubled as she realized that she didn't *want* Buford to go anywhere — she was enjoying his closeness. She couldn't pretend to herself that she wasn't attracted to him. In fact, she was afraid she was even more attracted to Buford than she'd ever been to Jonathan. Buford had a fantastic sense of humor like Jonathan, but where Jonathan was erratic and high-strung, always tense about one thing or another, Buford was straight-as-an-arrow sure, easygoing, and confident. Plus, he was a fellow actor, someone who shared her own interest, her love for the dramatic arts. And Buford was also so incredibly goodlooking. . . .

Lily clenched her teeth and made a move to rise, Buford or no Buford. Thinking about him this way was all wrong. She had to get out of the costume room before she let the magnetism between her and Buford erase her memory of all the wonderful times she and Jonathan had spent together, all they'd meant to each other. But she'd waited a moment too long. For the first time Lily noticed that she and Buford were now alone in the costume room. The rest of the cast had obviously made their selections and headed back to the stage for rehearsal. Buford had taken advantage of the lack of bystanders to move even closer to Lily.

"Um, we should probably, uh, get moving," Lily stuttered, her breath coming fast. "Rehearsal is probably starting. We wouldn't want to be late."

Buford nodded. "We have a minute," he assured her calmly. "I just want to ask you something, Lily."

111

"W-what?" she squeaked.

Buford held her eyes for a long moment, his own eyes so warm and eloquent he almost didn't need words to speak to her. Lily was terrified that he was going to kiss her. His eyes told her he wanted to, and she knew that if he did, the entire battle would be lost. She knew his kiss would completely melt her. But what then? . . . How could she ever face Jonathan again?

To her relief — mixed in with a little disappointment — Buford didn't kiss her. Instead he surprised Lily by saying hopefully, "I wanted to know if you'd like to meet me at the Welcome Dance tomorrow night. If you're free, that is."

Lily smiled broadly. She was willing to agree to nearly anything Buford asked in order to escape from the costume room unkissed. And meeting Buford at the dance wasn't exactly an awful price to pay. "Sure, I'd love to meet you at the dance," she replied, her pleasure as sincere as her relief.

"Good!" Buford was smiling now, too, but the look of serious purpose didn't leave his eyes. Lily had a sudden feeling that she might only have won the first round of her fight for self-control where Buford was concerned. But she didn't have time to think about round two. Now they really were late for rehearsal.

"Let's go," she suggested. Buford jumped to his feet and reached down to give her a hand. In a few seconds they had recovered all their costume pieces, the eyeglasses included, and were at the door of the costume room. Lily turned to switch off the light before she closed the door behind her. As she paused for a moment, looking out over the rainbow created by the hundreds of costumes, she made a new rule for herself. She could meet Buford at the dance the next night, but she couldn't kiss him. Not even just a tiny peck hello or good-bye. She couldn't kiss Buford, period. Not at the dance, not ever. Thinking of Jonathan, Lily crossed her heart in her imagination. Now *this* rule she absolutely would keep.

Chapter
10

Charlotte bent over to dig at the bottom of her overflowing locker. It was lucky that first period didn't start for ten minutes, she thought ruefully. It would take at least that long to un-earth her chemistry notebook and a sharp pencil!

Her messy locker was probably Charlotte's deepest, darkest secret. She guessed her polished, organized exterior led most people to imagine she was almost compulsively neat. Anyone who really knew her well knew that she was very disciplined but allowed herself one tiny flaw — her messy school locker. Although when you got right down to it, Charlotte thought as she put a triumphant hand on her calculator, while she'd made a lot of *friends* at Kennedy since her move the year before from Alabama, they weren't really *close* friends. Roxanne was the only person Char felt she could completely confide in. And even Rox didn't know how much Charlotte's forbidden feelings for Vince had been tearing her apart lately. Rox was the last person she could share that with.

Char let out a small sigh as she straightened up, one slender arm full of books. With her free hand she shut her locker and gave her long blonde curls a smoothing pat. It had been relatively easy at first, denying her attraction to Vince. Charlotte had put her friendship for Roxanne first, and besides, there were plenty of other cute boys in Rose Hill. But there were none like Vince, and the more Charlotte came to know him, the more it hurt to push him away.

Just don't think about it, Char advised herself, frowning sternly. Then her face brightened. Roxanne was strolling in Charlotte's direction. The two girls often met before school and their morning chat was one of the highlights of the day for Charlotte. Because of the Welcome Dance that evening, her day was going to be exceptionally busy, so Charlotte resolved to fully enjoy these few moments of relaxation. Roxanne would provide plenty of entertainment to distract her from her worries and responsibilities.

" 'Morning, Rox!" Char greeted her friend cheerfully. "What a great dress. I love it. But I can't believe your mom lets you leave the house like that!" she added, teasing. Char genuinely did admire Roxanne's flashy wardrobe, even though she personally would never dare wear a short — very short — green ultrasuede dress to school, or anywhere else. No skirt Charlotte owned fell above her knees. The dress had "Rox" written all over it, though. It was Charlotte's proud opinion that her friend was the most sensationally striking girl at Kennedy High.

Roxanne, meanwhile, had sniffed slightly at Charlotte's compliment. "Frankly," Rox said dryly, "my mother wouldn't care if I left the house wearing a plastic garbage bag belted at the waist with plastic twist ties. She's not exactly up in the morning making me a bag lunch, if you know what I mean."

Charlotte made a sympathetic half smile, half frown, wishing she'd kept her mouth shut. Roxanne didn't talk about her family much, but from what Char could see, Rox's divorced mother wasn't exactly attentive and affectionate. Charlotte knew she was very lucky in comparison. She had two loving, supportive parents, where Rox was nearly an emotional orphan.

Charlotte looked for a tactful way to change the subject. She had so much on her mind what with the dance that night, it wasn't hard to come up with a fresh topic. "Speaking of clothes, I haven't even begun to think about what I'm going to wear to the dance." Char rolled her eyes. "How about you, Rox?"

Rox shrugged negligently. "I bought a dress at Foxy Lady," she said in the distasteful tone she often used when referring to the store her mother's boyfriend, George Royce, owned. "Now that it's fall, he's starting to carry more evening wear in addition to that pricey lingerie. It's blue, with a low back and sequins. Actually, it's very cute," Roxanne had to admit. Then she smiled wickedly. "And I got a twenty-five-percent discount. Old

116

George is good for something besides bossing me and Torrey around!"

"Well, that's good," Charlotte said sincerely. She took it as a good sign that Roxanne should say anything positive about George, even as a joke. "Think how much easier things would be at home if you started getting along better with George. Wouldn't that make your mother happy?"

"Hmmm," Rox mumbled vaguely. Her grim expression warned Charlotte that once again she was treading on uncomfortable ground. It looked like it was time to change the subject again.

The two had been wandering in the direction of the girls' room for their habitual morning makeup check. Now Charlotte spotted Stacy, Lily, and Frankie in a huddle by Stacy's locker just a few yards farther down the hall. Instead of entering the bathroom, she detoured to join them, with Roxanne trailing somewhat disinterestedly behind her. "Just the people I wanted to see!" Char announced brightly. "Or at least, you're the next best thing. Have any of you seen Josh, Zack, or Greg around this morning?"

Charlotte couldn't wait until lunch period that day when the chairs in the Little Theater would finally be moved. That would mean one less thing to worry about. As preoccupied as she may have been with dance details, though, Charlotte couldn't help noticing that Frankie, Stacy, and Lily jumped apart somewhat guiltily when she and Roxanne approached. Frankie blushed furiously, and all three wore awkward, embarrassed expressions. Who were they talking about? *Me?* Charlotte wondered, perplexed.

117

She was even more befuddled when a few seconds later Lily and Stacy dashed off without even saying hello. "Um, we have to stop by the, uh, gym. . . . My cheerleading uniform . . ." Stacy muttered. Lily just waved and then they were lost in the milling stream of students.

Charlotte blankly watched them go. "Did Rox and I chase them away?" she joked to Frankie.

"Of course not!" Frankie assured her, too quickly. "They just have things to do. And that reminds me. . . ." Frankie hesitated, the pink spots on her pale cheeks deepening. Not meeting Charlotte's eyes, Frankie cleared her throat and continued. "Josh asked me to let you know that he's really sorry but he — he can't help you move the seats in the theater today. His assistant at the radio station is . . . sick. So Josh has to stick around at WKND during lunch."

"Don't worry, I understand completely," Char said warmly. "The radio is his priority, just like the dance is mine. I wouldn't want him to short-change the WKND audience!"

"Good." Frankie appeared relieved. Then she took a deep breath and blurted out, "And I think — sorry again — I think Stacy was saying something about Greg maybe having a conference with the student government advisor during lunch today. But I'm not sure."

"Oh." Charlotte didn't want to let on that she was disappointed. After all, the boys had their own responsibilities. "Well, that wouldn't be too much of a problem for me. I think I'll have plenty of help."

"I hope so." Frankie turned her wrist and read

her watch in an exaggerated fashion. "Oops! Speaking of Josh, I was supposed to meet him at WKND five minute ago to . . . to. . . . 'Bye!"

An instant later Frankie and her yellow corduroy jumper had disappeared into the crowd. Roxanne and Charlotte were left standing alone, pressed against the row of lockers by the momentum of the hall traffic. Char frowned slightly. She felt as if she had water in her ears or the sun in her eyes or something. Was it her imagination or had that just been a very strange encounter? Ordinarily Lily, Stacy, and Frankie were as happy to see her as she was to see them. Ordinarily they'd all have hung around together until the very last minute, when they'd have to sprint to make it to homeroom on time.

Now that Charlotte thought about it, though, her girlfriends — with the exception of Roxanne — had been acting a little cool toward her all week. The last time she sat with Lily, Frankie, and Stacy in the cafeteria during lunch, they'd pulled a vanishing act similar to the one Charlotte had just witnessed. And a few nights ago when she called Stacy about their American history assignment, she'd thought she heard some whispering going on in the background before Stacy's brother got back on the phone to tell Char his sister wasn't at home. Or had that been Char's imagination, too?

Charlotte blinked a few times, refocusing on the present moment. Roxanne was watching her with an odd gleam in her eyes. "Is anything the matter?" Rox asked in a candy-sweet tone.

Char shrugged. "I'm really not sure," she said

119

thoughtfully. "Maybe. Do you think we have time for a quick trip to the bathroom?"

Roxanne glanced at the institutional-looking clock on the corridor wall. "Three minutes, long enough for a quick visit."

"Then let's go."

Charlotte was glad to see that the nearest girls' room was empty. The other primpers must already have concluded their morning inspections and headed to class. Positioning themselves in front of the mirror, Char and Roxanne opened their purses simultaneously. Rox whipped out a mauve lip pencil while Char fiddled with her tortoiseshell hairbrush. "Roxanne?" she said tentatively.

"Hmmm?"

Charlotte hesitated, unsure of how to put her hazy concerns into words. "Do you think the girls — Stacy, Lily, and Frankie, I mean — are . . . *mad* at me for some reason?"

Roxanne finished carefully lining her lips before she answered Charlotte's question. "Mad?" she repeated, sounding mystified. "What makes you think that?"

"I don't know. They seemed kind of in a hurry to go somewhere else the minute we walked up just now," Charlotte explained as she adjusted the collar of her pastel floral-print dress. "And I've been getting that impression all week."

Rox replaced her lip pencil and then, tossing her tawny hair over one shoulder, began brushing it briskly. "I think you're imagining things," she told Charlotte. "Really. I didn't notice anything." Roxanne studied Charlotte appraisingly. "Why would they be mad at you anyhow? Could you give me even one logical reason?"

Char's blue eyes widened with innocent puzzlement. "I don't know. Maybe I offended them in some way. But how? Did I do or say something wrong? I would never mean to, but maybe I did. I just don't know!"

Roxanne reached over to pat Charlotte consolingly on the shoulder. "Don't worry Char. *You* could never say or do anything to offend anybody." Charlotte was too distraught to pick up on the sharp edge to Roxanne's kind tone. "Everybody is wild about you. So just relax. Any problem between you and them is all in your mind. Believe me."

Charlotte wanted to believe her. It was certainly more pleasant than believing that her friends were mad at her for some mysterious reason. "You're probably right," Char acknowledged, her expression hopeful. "I guess I'm just sort of hyper about the dance tonight. I'm so nervous — I really want everything to go perfectly. This wouldn't be the first molehill I've made into a mountain lately!"

Roxanne laughed as she zipped her pocketbook shut with a flourish. "Well, make it right back into a molehill, and let's get a move on before we get homeroom tardies!"

Since they had the same homeroom, the two girls headed down the hall together. As they went, Roxanne gave Charlotte another vibrant, reassuring smile. "Lighten up, DeVries!" she teased.

"I will," Charlotte promised. "And thanks,

Rox. I guess I was just getting worked up over nothing."

Roxanne was still smiling, although the light didn't quite reach her shadowed eyes. "What are friends for?" she said blithely.

What are friends for is right, Charlotte thought, her spirits lifting. Her mood improved with every step she took. Rox was right, there was nothing to worry about. She knew she hadn't done anything to warrant her friends' disapproval, and they would never turn against her without having a very good reason. Rox was right, Charlotte repeated silently to herself with somewhat forced certainty. Everything was fine. . . . Wasn't it?

It was all Roxanne could do to keep from leaping into the air and clicking her heels together as she hurried to homeroom alongside Charlotte. But no, she had to keep her triumph to herself. Not a soul, least of all Charlotte, could know that she wasn't the loyal and true friend she pretended to be. But she could risk just a smile. Rox's lips curved wickedly as she recalled Charlotte's distress in the girls' room. If Char only knew how pathetic she'd looked and sounded! She was such a little Girl Scout. "Did I offend somebody? Did I say something wrong?" It really was a laugh. There was Charlotte, worried sick about hurting the feelings of stupid Lily, Frankie, and Stacy, when meanwhile she'd carelessly stabbed in the back the person who'd made the mistake of considering herself Charlotte's best friend. Yes, you offended somebody, Rox accused Char silently. You offended me. And no one gets the

122

chance to make that mistake twice.

Roxanne was still smiling secretively as she and Charlotte breezed into homeroom, only seconds before the bell rang. Roxanne ignored the teacher's slight scowl, concentrating instead on taking a seat with as much of a flourish as she could manage. She was pleased to see at least five boys practically fall out of their chairs as she crossed her long legs and adjusted the hem of her dress.

Roxanne bit back a bitter laugh. Now she was thinking ahead, picturing Charlotte at the Little Theater during lunch period later, patiently waiting for all the guys she'd recruited to show up and help her out. Did she have a surprise coming! From Frankie, Stacy, and Lily's behavior, it was plain to see that Jana had sounded the alarm, just as Roxanne had expected she would. Sooner or later the word might even filter through the grapevine to the Kennedy men. Vince himself would hear what kind of girl Charlotte really was. Then he would be sorry he'd tossed Roxanne aside.

Rox examined her sharp, perfectly polished fingernails. She didn't doubt that Vince would come crawling back to her as soon as he saw the error of his ways. Well, she'd let him crawl. And when he was good and humbled, and when Charlotte was cast out from the crowd and maybe even forced to resign from her position as Kennedy High's student activities director because of her plummeting popularity, then Roxanne would make her move and take what was rightfully hers.

Chapter
11

Vince tipped back in his chair and placed his heavy Timberland boots on top of Daniel's desk with a clunk. "The whole newspaper is great, really professional," he observed. "But I've got to admit, I especially like the way the Wilderness Club calendar turned out. You did a great job. I don't think I've seen *The Red and the Gold* look better."

"Really?" Daniel removed the Wayfarer sunglasses which had been pushed back on his head. He fidgeted with them, opening and closing them in time to the beat of the WKND noontime new music show. "I'm glad you liked it. I've gotten a lot of great feedback — a lot. It's good to hear, I have to admit."

Vince nodded. "I'd say you and your whole staff are a big success. It looks like you picked all the right people to back you up."

Daniel narrowed his intense green eyes. "I did,

didn't I?" Glancing over at Tim Shannon, the junior varsity sports editor, who was bent over a desk on the far side of the newspaper office, Daniel lowered his voice. "But I haven't told you the whole secret of my success, Vince," he said, his expression grim.

Vince raised his heavy eyebrows, curious. "What do you mean?"

Daniel snapped his sunglasses shut and tossed them onto the desk. As he crossed his arms over his chest, his frown deepened. He hadn't forgotten the conversation he'd had with Sara Gates earlier in the week, the day the newspaper first came out. That was, if you could even call it a conversation. It had been more like an explosion on Sara's part. But Daniel had to acknowledge that he deserved every harsh word she'd thrown at him. Everything Sara had said was only too true. But what was he supposed to do now? Was it possible to think about turning over a new leaf when the situation with Lin hadn't changed? Daniel didn't know. He looked at his good friend Vince with a speculative eye. Maybe he would have some ideas.

"I got some fine work out of my staff," Daniel explained, "but not by treating them with the respect they deserve. I totally bullied them for the entire time we were working on this issue." He briefed Vince on his encounter with Sara. "Man, when she lit into me like that, it really made me stop and take a look at myself, at what I've been doing, you know? And I didn't like what I saw any better than she did."

Vince shook his head in sympathy. "Sometimes it takes somebody else, someone you don't even know that well, to show you what a jerk you are." He made a wry face. "That didn't come out the way I meant. You're not *that* big of a jerk. . . ."

Daniel grinned. "Call a spade a spade, DiMase."

"Okay, you're a jerk." Vince leaned over and punched Daniel lightly on the arm. "But you know what I mean. Sometimes someone who's not in on what's going on in your life can see it objectively when you can't."

"That's just it," Daniel conceded. "She sort of did, and then I did. Look at my life objectively, I mean. And like I said, I didn't like what I saw. Do you think being depressed over Lin has turned me into a monster?"

Daniel was only half joking as he asked the question. Vince considered it seriously. "Maybe a little. It has to have an effect." Vince's normally good-natured expression twisted into a somewhat bitter smile. "You know, I'm right there with you on this. I'm not exactly in great shape these days myself. This whole deal with Char, or rather the lack thereof. . . ." Vince shrugged sadly. "It's definitely a bummer."

Daniel pounded his fist fiercely on the desktop. "It's just so frustrating." he exclaimed. "What really kills me is that I just can't *do* anything. Lin's parents don't approve of me because I'm not Asian and that's that. No matter what Lin might or might not feel, we're stuck. I just can't reach her."

Vince nodded in complete understanding. "That's exactly how I'd describe my relationship with Charlotte! It's like we're stuck at the starting

126

line. I know she likes me, and I'm wild about her, of course. But she doesn't want to get involved because she's afraid it would hurt Roxanne's feelings. I admire her loyalty and all, but it's keeping us apart when it shouldn't. Man, what happened between me and Rox is ancient history now."

Daniel laughed sarcastically. "We're pretty pathetic, huh?"

"No kidding!" Vince forced a smile that was more sad than amused. Then a gleam returned to his eyes. "But maybe that's our whole problem. We've been sitting around for weeks feeling sorry for ourselves, waiting for Lin and Charlotte to put us out of our misery one way or another." Vince pointed a finger at Daniel. "What we both need to do is to do something concrete to get our romantic lives back in gear."

Daniel nodded. "Sounds like a good idea," he said slowly. "But do what?"

Vince looked stumped. "Hmmm. Good question. I don't know what exactly, but take some kind of action. Anything has to be better than moping around and stewing in our own bad feelings until we blow up at people."

Daniel thought deeply, his pale forehead wrinkled in concentration. *Action, action. . . .* He pictured himself pulling into Lin's driveway, the tires of his car squealing. He'd bang the front door down and then demand that her parents allow them to see each other. There was action for you! Daniel thought with bitter humor. That's what he'd do if he were an actor in a movie about his life. But here in the real world, he still felt . . . *stuck*.

Just then Daniel realized that Vince was getting quickly to his feet. "Hey, where are you going?" he asked his friend.

"I just got an inspiration," Vince announced, his deep voice suddenly full of purpose. He grinned, looking nervous but determined. "You want to see some action, Tackett? Here goes!"

"What . . . ?"

Vince was already halfway to the door. "I'll tell you all about it later — if it works."

"So long. Good luck!"

The door swung shut behind Vince with a hollow click. Daniel noticed that at some point Tim had disappeared as well. He had the office all to himself — just him and his gloomy thoughts. Daniel sat for a full five minutes staring straight at the whitewashed wall, his eye tracing all the spiderweblike cracks in the paint. Then he tugged open the desk drawer and pulled out a new yellow legal pad and a blue ballpoint pen. He smoothed a hand over the top sheet and sat unmoving, his hand poised to write.

Dear Sara, he finally began. He rubbed his eyes, searching for the right way to apologize, then decided that short and sweet was probably best. *I'm genuinely sorry for the way I've been treating you and the rest of* The Red and the Gold *staff. You're a valuable part of things, and I hope you'll give me a second chance and stay with the newspaper. It needs you, and so do I. Thanks for telling me how you feel — I promise to be as honest with you in the future. Daniel.*

Daniel tore the page from the pad and folded

it carefully, then placed it in an envelope with Sara's name on the outside and tucked it into his backpack. He'd drop it off at the message center before lunch period was over; they'd page Sara over the loudspeaker along with the other message recipients, and she could pick up the letter later that day.

The clock over the door informed Daniel that he had fifteen minutes until the end of lunch. He ran a hand restlessly through his shaggy dark hair. Fifteen minutes to compose a second letter, he thought, feeling almost scared. This one was going to be a lot harder to write, and a lot longer than the first. The right words were going to be even more difficult to find, but he knew he had to try.

Daniel took a deep breath and picked up the pen again. He confronted the legal pad, willing his hand to stop shaking. Instead of his usual scrawl, he printed each letter distinctly. DEAR LIN. . . .

Charlotte felt very small standing alone in the left aisle of the echoing, empty Little Theater. She peered at her watch one more time. Maybe it was fast, she couldn't help hoping. Maybe it wasn't really fifteen minutes into lunch, with not one person in sight to help her move the seats out of the way for the dance that night. But inside Charlotte knew it was just wishful thinking. The fact was that none of the guys who'd promised to help had shown up. Not one. It was like being stood up for the prom.

Char bit her lip and scanned the dusky theater apprehensively. There had to be at least a million chairs there. It was an impossible job for one person, especially when that one person was wearing heels and a new dress. But she didn't have any alternative; she'd have to start moving them herself.

Gingerly rolling up her sleeves, Charlotte approached the first seat. She gripped the worn, cushioned seatback and yanked at it. It didn't budge. Bending over, she examined the seat's metal underpinnings. To her dismay, the chair looked like it was actually attached to the one next to it. Practically on her hands and knees, Charlotte crept into the row of seats, checking each one in turn. She was right, the seats *were* clamped tightly together — in groups of *four*! Even if she managed to loosen the large bolts attaching them to the floor, she'd never be able to move the four-chair units out of the way.

"Wasn't that why I wanted boys to help me in the first place?" Charlotte asked out loud, her voice cracking with irritation and disappointment. She straightened up and dusted off her dress with sharp, angry swipes. Then she kicked ineffectually at one of the chairs with her right foot. A stinging pain darted through her big toe. Char bent over to squeeze it through the shiny leather of her shoe, her eyes suddenly brimming with tears. It was bad enough that all her girlfriends were being mean to her for some reason, but now the boys had deserted her as well. She couldn't move the chairs and therefore the Welcome Dance, her first project as student activities director, was going to be a total flop. The whole school year might as well be written off right now! Charlotte slumped down into one of the faded theater seats and burst into full-fledged sobs of frustration.

It made her feel a little better to cry, so Char didn't make any effort to stop her tears. There was nobody around to see her anyhow. She might as well cry for the rest of the lunch period.

"Do you need some help, Charlotte?" The kind, male voice coming from somewhere in the rear of the theater gave Charlotte a jolt. With a shaky hand she brushed away her tears and turned to gaze, blinking, up the aisle. A tall figure was silhouetted against the light from the lobby beyond the open double doors. It was Vince.

He was standing hesitantly in the doorway, but when he saw Charlotte's miserable expression, he started down the aisle toward her with long strides. Humiliated, Charlotte turned forward again in her seat and buried her face in her hands. Of all the people who could have walked in and seen her in such a state, it had to be Vince! In a way it was really fitting. From the start Charlotte had suspected that Vince was a real-life knight in shining armor, the kind of guy who would always be there when you needed him. She'd known lots of chivalrous southern gentlemen when she'd lived in Alabama, but for most of them that kind of behavior was part of an act. With Vince, Charlotte knew it was genuine unselfishness. Still, she was nothing less than mortified to be caught crying like a four-year-old. She pressed her fists against her tear-filled eyes, wishing she could melt into the floor like the Wicked Witch of the West in *The Wizard of Oz*. But she was cornered.

"Char, what's the matter?" Vince asked, his voice low and tender.

Charlotte had managed to stem the flood of her tears, but when Vince slipped into the next seat and leaned toward her, his eyes glowing with concern, she started crying all over again. Inside she knew she should keep her distance from Vince — if she let him comfort her now, it would be even harder to stay away next time. But right then she needed him. Roxanne or no Roxanne, Charlotte needed Vince's strength and understanding. She threw her arms around Vince's neck. In an instant he had wrapped her up in a warm, loving hug.

"There, there," he said into her hair, patting her back awkwardly. "It's going to be okay."

Charlotte shook her head. She really didn't think it *was* going to be okay. But when Vince lifted her face to his and began kissing the tears one by one off her cheeks, she was ready to change her mind. Nothing could really seem so awful when she was with Vince. Whatever else might be going wrong, all her instincts told her that what she and Vince had — could have — was right.

Charlotte's arms were still around Vince's neck. Now she twined her fingers in his hair, staring deep into his eyes. Vince stared back. "Hi," Char whispered with a shy smile.

Vince bent forward and lightly kissed the tip of her nose. "Hi, yourself."

It suddenly occurred to Charlotte that Vince's showing up in the Little Theater at just that moment couldn't simply be a coincidence. "Why did you come here?" she wondered.

Vince held Char a little bit closer. "Well, for one thing, I wanted to volunteer my chair-moving assistance." He looked around him for the first time at the deserted theater and smiled crookedly. "It looks like you need it more than I thought."

Charlotte tried to smile, too. "You can say that again," she acknowledged with a sniffle.

Vince's expression had become serious again. "But that's not the main reason I'm here. The main reason is that I — we — it's been long enough, Charlotte." His hands tightened on her slender shoulders. The warmth from his strong fingers burned through the thin fabric of her dress. "It's been a long time since I broke up with Roxanne. I want to be with you, and I don't want to wait anymore."

A spark of pleasure shot through Charlotte. She'd heard about people tingling from their heads to their toes, but she'd never felt that way before now. She was sure that Vince's words were the most beautiful she would ever hear. "I want to be with you, too, Vince," she said with all her heart. But even though she was beaming with happiness, Charlotte was still anxious. Being with Vince was like a dream come true and everything might work out wonderfully for them, but there was still Roxanne and her feelings to deal with.

"Then there's nothing stopping us?" Vince asked. He waited eagerly for her answer.

"Well . . ." Charlotte paused. The disappointment in Vince's eyes made her drop her own. "Roxanne — "

"We can't let her keep us apart forever," Vince pointed out urgently.

"I know," Char admitted, "but she's still my best friend, Vince. And under the circumstances I think I owe her an explanation. At least let me talk it over with her. I just don't want us getting together to come as a shock, a betrayal, to her." She tried to look at the bright side, for Vince's sake as much as for her own. "I'm sure once Roxanne understands how much you and I care for one another, she'll be happy for us. You know, she's really a very generous person."

Vince smoothed Charlotte's silky hair back from her forehead. "I hope so," was all he said.

"I know so," Char declared with certainty.

"So. . . ." He grinned at her with the slightly embarrassed expression of a boy about to ask a girl out on a date for the first time. "I guess it's too late to line you up for the Welcome Dance tonight, huh?"

"Well, actually I *was* kind of planning to be there." They both laughed. "How about we just meet there?" she suggested.

"Promise me a dance, if you can squeeze one in, that is."

"I'd love to."

"Great." Vince gave Char a fast hug. "I think I'm the happiest guy in the world."

Charlotte smiled, blushing. She knew exactly what Vince meant; she was feeling the same sort of dizzy euphoria. Then suddenly she came back

134

to earth. She directed Vince's attention to the sea of chairs around them, all still very firmly bolted to the floor of the Little Theater. "Don't speak too soon," she warned him. "Happiness has a price. In this case, the price is a couple hundred chairs' worth of sweaty labor!"

"No problem." Vince stood up and reached into his back pockets, withdrawing a pair of pliers and a sturdy wrench, which he displayed proudly to Charlotte. "I came armed." Vince winked. "We Wilderness Clubbers are always prepared for an emergency!" He scanned the chairs with a practiced eye. "With teamwork, we should be able to get these all moved in about an hour. What do you say? Are you game?"

Char nodded, sniffling away the last of her tears. With Vince's help, she did feel as if she could accomplish almost anything. "Let's go for it," she said enthusiastically.

Vince spread his jacket on the floor for Charlotte to kneel on, and they set to work on the chairs together.

Chapter
12

"This isn't *really* a date," Lily said out loud to herself as she stood in front of her open closet deciding what to wear to the Welcome Dance, which started in an hour. "I'm just meeting Buford at school — it's not like he's picking me up at my house or buying me a corsage or anything."

Well, if it isn't a real date, then why haven't you said anything about it to Frankie or Stacy? an inner voice asked Lily. *Or to Jonathan?*

Lily yanked the nearest dress off its hanger and tossed it onto her bed. She opted not to answer the inner voice's question, mostly because she didn't have a good answer, or at least an answer that wouldn't contradict her "this isn't really a date" philosophy. It was easier, and safer, to stick with the facts of the situation and not look too closely at the feelings.

And the facts were that the dance started in an

hour and her dress needed ironing, her hair needed washing, and her fingernails needed filing . . . and that was just the start! This might not really be a date, but Lily still wanted to look the best she could.

The phone rang just as Lily was starting to run the water in the bathtub. She dashed out of the bathroom and down the hall, grabbing the phone on the nightstand in her parents' bedroom before the third ring. "Hello?" she said breathlessly.

Lily was expecting to hear Buford's voice and her lips curved in an expectant, nervous smile. Maybe he was going to offer to pick her up after all. Should she accept? Would that threaten the dance's not-really-a-date status?

But it wasn't Buford on the other end. It was Jonathan. "Hi, Lil, it's me," he said, sounding overjoyed to find her at home. Lily's smile faded and her already-pale face whitened. *Jonathan.* Of course, she thought dully, feeling a little dizzy as she sank down onto the bed, her shoulders slumping. Of course, Jonathan was the boy who *should* be calling her. He was her boyfriend, not Buford. He was supposed to be the one on her mind. But he wasn't. She'd been thinking and dreaming about Buford for the past week and longer, and she had a very pronounced feeling that the pre-occupation was mutual. She could pretend that the dance tonight didn't mean anything, wouldn't lead to anything, but she was just fooling herself.

"Uh, hi, Jonathan," Lily finally responded, her voice weak. She stuttered through a few automatic questions — How are you? How is school? — while her mind continued running in circles.

Did she have the courage to bring up the subject of Buford and/or the possibility of dating other people right now? Would she ever have the courage? Part of Lily was ready to go for it, but the other part was far too chicken. I'll compromise, Lily silently decided at last. I'll find out what kind of mood Jonathan is in and follow his lead. Maybe he'd be more "up" than he was in their last few conversations. Maybe he'd even like the idea of retracting that silly promise. Lily didn't admit to herself how unlikely that was.

"So, what are you doing home on a Friday night, Lil?" Jonathan asked, his voice teasing. "No big date?"

Lily forced a brittle laugh. She knew Jonathan was joking. If she even hinted that she planned to spend the evening with one particular boy, Jonathan would completely flip out. "Actually, there's a big fall dance at school tonight," she informed him, sounding as offhand as she could. "Everyone will be there. I thought I'd stop by for a while. You know, hang out with the gang, maybe stop by the sub shop later. Now that I think about it, it's been a while since I OD'd on their extra-greasy onion rings!"

Jonathan heaved such a big sigh that Lily thought she could almost feel it through the telephone. "Gee, that sounds like fun," he said wistfully. "I'd give absolutely anything to be there. Seriously." Jonathan sighed again, and this time the sound was almost painful. Lily heard his whole aching heart in it. "Oh, what's the point of putting on an act with you?" Jonathan declared dismally. "I don't know why I was even trying. I guess I was just automatically using the happy-go-lucky-freshman voice I use with everyone else." Jonathan hesitated. When he continued, his tone was even more emotional. "I miss you so much, Lily. I miss the crowd and Kennedy High and Rose Hill and even the sub shop. Am I crazy or what?"

"No, you're not crazy," Lily told him sincerely. "Hey, you've spent your whole life here, Jonathan. This is your home. It's totally natural to miss it, and to miss your friends." She swallowed, wishing away the guilt that was weighing her down. She wanted to mean what she was about to say next. "And your friends miss you, too. *I* miss you."

"You really do?" It was clear Jonathan needed as much reassurance as Lily could give him. "Do you miss me as much as I miss you?"

"Uh, yeah," Lily hedged. "I mean, how much do you miss me?"

"A lot. Even more than I thought I would." Lily was silent. Here was her chance to admit that she did miss Jonathan, but somewhat less than she thought she would. She couldn't. This obviously wasn't the time to discuss her changing feelings. Jonathan needed her support and as a friend she owed him that much. Lily just let Jonathan talk. "It's this whole college thing, Lil," he began. "I'm really not sure it's for me. I mean, I can't seem to get used to things here at Penn, and I don't know if I ever will."

Lily sat back on her parents' bed, tucking their blue-and-green quilt around her knees. She might as well get comfortable; it looked as if she'd be on the phone for quite a while. "In what way?" she asked. "In what way can't you get used to Penn?"

"In a lot of ways. Like, there's the dorm," Jonathan said, citing an example. "It's me and about a thousand other freshman guys. Most of them are nice and all — we hang out together and go to meals and parties and stuff — but I don't feel like they're my friends. I mean, they're just not Jeremy or Eric or Greg or Matt — "

Lily interrupted him. "Well, you have to give them time," she pointed out reasonably. "You didn't become best pals with any of the Rose Hill guys overnight, either."

"Yeah, I suppose that's true," Jonathan acknowledged, but he didn't sound one-hundred-percent convinced. In typical style, he switched gears abruptly. "And then there're my classes. Man, I study about twelve times as hard as I ever did at Kennedy, and it seems like it's all I can do just to keep my head above water."

"Penn is a pretty competitive school," Lily reminded him. "Only people who are really smart even get in there in the first place. You could hardly expect to cruise along as easily as you did at Kennedy. I bet the professors expect a lot from you."

"You can say that again," Jonathan declared. "I've only been here a month, and I've already taken two tests and written four papers!"

"Ugh," Lily exclaimed sympathetically. "That *is* pretty rough. But the work'll probably get easier as time goes along. That's the way that kind of thing usually works."

"I just don't know." Jonathan refused to be consoled. While he'd been talking about academics, his tone had grown calmer. Now he started to sound upset again. "Lil, it's not just the guys in the dorm or my classes. It's everything. College is such a big place, you know? I just don't feel like I'll ever belong here."

Lily sighed, sad and worried but determined to talk Jonathan into a more positive frame of mind. She could do it if she took the time. And she wanted to take the time, more than anything. The only problem was that the dance started — the dance! Lily jumped up from the bed, the phone nearly flying out of her hand. She'd left the water running, and by now the bathroom was probably flooded!

"Jonathan, I have to run and turn off the water — I was about to get in the tub when you called. Can you hold on a minute?"

The short trip to the bathroom and back gave Lily a few much-needed moments to think. If she wanted to get to the dance on time — if she wanted to get to the dance at all — she'd have to cut short her conversation with Jonathan. It probably wouldn't be the end of the world. Jonathan would understand, and they could always talk tomorrow. And after all, Buford was waiting for her. . . .

But even as she rationalized about going to the dance, Lily knew that her feelings weren't the point. Maybe this wasn't the best time Jonathan could have chosen to call, but the fact was he'd called and he needed to talk to her. He needed cheering up, now. And whatever might be happening inside her, whatever might be happening to her love for Jonathan, Lily knew she'd always care very deeply for him. No matter what else, he was still one of her closest friends. If the tables were turned and she had turned to Jonathan only to get put off because he had a dance to get ready for, her heart would have broken. She couldn't do that to him. He meant too much to her. And if Buford was waiting, well, he could wait for a little while longer. She wasn't going to any dance tonight.

Lily trotted back into her parents' bedroom. She made herself comfortable under the fluffy quilt as she picked up the receiver. "You still there, Jonathan?"

"Of course," he said gruffly. "I'm not going anywhere."

"Good," Lily said, her voice warm and caring. "Neither am I."

Chapter
13

Backstage at the Little Theater, Charlotte sank down into a metal folding chair, exhausted. She couldn't believe how beat she was. And it was only ten o'clock! The Welcome Dance was just starting to roll. Char felt as if she'd peaked hours ago. She'd been in the Little Theater since the final bell that afternoon. She hadn't gone home after school, and she'd even missed the football game that evening, although from all reports Kennedy High's victory had been the most exciting one yet.

Well, the sacrifices were worth it, she thought with a tired rush of pride. The disc jockey she'd lined up in lieu of a live band to save money was playing fantastic music, and the dance floor, which earlier that day had been a theater full of chairs, was packed with swaying bodies. With the help of a couple of kids from the AV Club, Charlotte had just finished setting up the screen for the football video; it would start during a break in the music in a few minutes. The decorations and refreshments had received high praise, and even the chaperones — the junior class advisors, guidance counselors, and the new vice principal, Ms. Burling — were having fun. Charlotte's first event as student activities director was an unqualified success.

Well, maybe not *unqualified,* Char mused. She put a hand to her forehead and rubbed her throbbing temples. Face it, she thought sadly: The person who put the most work into this dumb dance, the person who deserves more than anybody else to have a good time — *me* — isn't. She was trying her hardest to relax and enjoy herself. She had taken a few breaks to join the rest of the crowd. After looking in vain for Vince, she'd spotted Frankie dancing with Josh. Charlotte hadn't forgotten the way the girls had acted toward her that morning, but after her discussion with Roxanne, she'd talked herself into believing there hadn't been anything behind it. So she'd approached Frankie optimistically, expecting a friendly reception. When Charlotte had joked about cutting in on Frankie's dance with Josh, though, Frankie had whirled her boyfriend around and danced off with him without even saying hello. The next couple Charlotte stumbled across, Stacy and football-hero Zack, behaved in much the same fashion — before Char even had a chance to say hello.

Charlotte had retreated backstage, hurt and mystified. There was only one thing keeping her going at this point, and that was the memory of her lunch with Vince. Her cheeks turned bright pink just at the thought of the way his strong arms had felt as they'd encircled her. Vince had probably arrived at the dance by now — and any minute he might come backstage looking for her. Charlotte had wanted to talk to Roxanne before she saw Vince again, but she hadn't bumped into her friend since they parted before school that morning. Char wasn't really looking forward to it — what she had to say was bound to be difficult for both girls — but it was now or never. Once that was over with, Charlotte would be able to freely spend the rest of the evening with Vince.

Just a few more minutes of rest and then I'll find Roxanne, Char promised herself as she let her heavy eyelids droop. If only she hadn't worn her new black heels! she thought. Then her feet wouldn't be aching so badly. But the shoes did look nice with her dress. All in all, Charlotte was glad the lights in the Little Theater were so dim. That way no one could see how wrinkled her dress was after spending the day stowed in her cramped locker, or the shadows underneath her eyes.

Bruce Springsteen's "Tunnel of Love" faded to a close, and there were a few moments of relative quiet as the disc jockey, a senior named Mark Schmidt, chatted about the upcoming football video. Charlotte leaned forward, about to stand up and head out to look for Roxanne. Then she froze. She was hidden in her seat backstage, but through the closed curtain she could hear female voices talking none too quietly on the other side. And if she wasn't mistaken, they had mentioned her name.

". . . a pretty good dance, all things considered," one girl said begrudgingly.

"I know what you mean." The other girl's tone was knowing. "I can't believe this school could have elected a . . . *person* like that to such an important position!"

"Yeah. Uh, what exactly did you hear about her, anyway?" the first voice asked.

"*I* heard that Charlotte DeVries is basically a back-stabber," the second voice answered. "She stole Vince DiMase from Rox Easton, didn't she? It's all too obvious that she'll steal any boy who isn't tied down!"

"That's what I heard, too," the first voice confirmed. "She steals boyfriends, uses them, and then throws them away. And she's our activities director!"

"She probably organizes dances like this just so she can spy out the latest couples and break them up!" the other girl joked grimly.

Charlotte's hands were clenched tightly together in her lap. Her pretty face had gone white and then scarlet. She had heard lots of vicious rumors in her day, and she was probably guilty of passing along a few. But she'd never, ever heard one as terrible as this. And it was about *her*! Hot, confused tears sprang to Charlotte's eyes. Where could such a mean, miserable story have come from? Who would have said such horrible things about her? One thing was clear, however. It was no wonder Lily and Frankie and Stacy were giving her the cold shoulder. They must have heard the rumor and believed it. No wonder they had bolted when she'd teased about dancing with their boyfriends! Who could blame them?

Charlotte squeezed her eyes tightly shut, feeling the tears overflow and run down her flushed cheeks. At that moment she would have given just anything to be able to click the heels of her ruby slippers together three times and find herself back in her old room in Alabama. She'd known everybody at her old high school, and they'd known her. They'd grown up together. No one there would ever have dreamed of spreading — or believing — such a despicable story about her. Why had it happened here? What had she done to deserve it? Charlotte concentrated, trying to imagine a motive by looking at herself objectively, through a stranger's eyes. She supposed it was possible that someone could be jealous of her quick popularity and her involvement with the student government. After all, she'd only been at Kennedy for a semester, and already she was occupying an enviable social position. But starting a rumor like this one was more than just sour grapes. In was downright vicious.

The more Charlotte thought about it, the more angry she became. The gossip she'd just overheard had absolutely no basis in fact, and yet people were hearing it and passing it along. Her first instinct had been to stay backstage for the duration of her high school career. Now she realized that if the rumor was to be stopped — and it had to be — there was only one person who could do it. Charlotte herself.

Charlotte sniffled, wishing she had a tissue.

This wasn't a very appealing prospect. How should she go about it? Walk right up to Lily, Frankie, Stacy, and the others and beg them to believe all the rumors weren't true? It would be incredibly embarrassing, but it did look like the only option. If her friends heard the truth of the matter straight from Charlotte, they would have to believe her. And if they still weren't willing to give her the benefit of the doubt, then they weren't her friends. Period.

Charlotte jumped to her feet just as Vince burst through the opening in the curtain, his striped tie flapping. "Here you are!" he exclaimed, his eyes lighting up. "What are you hiding back here for? This is your dance, Char. You should be out there enjoying it!"

Char froze at Vince's entrance. It was all she could do now to force her lips to form a few simple words. "I was setting up the screen for the video," she explained, her voice barely more than a whisper.

At first Vince didn't notice Charlotte's red eyes and nose and her anxious tone. He moved toward her until he was near enough to put his hands on her shoulders and pull her close. "Char, did you have a chance to talk to Roxanne yet? Can we spend the rest of the evening together? I'd really love to dance with you." He grinned. "Out there with the rest of the world, not back here."

Charlotte stiffened. Abruptly she reached up and eased Vince's hands off her shoulders. Appearing at the dance with Vince now would only confirm the rumor! They couldn't risk it. "No, I didn't talk to Roxanne," she exclaimed breathlessly, her eyes wide. "But even if I had, I couldn't be seen with you!"

Vince's smile dissolved. "What do you mean?" he asked hoarsely, his expression strained and fearful. "What's happened?"

"Haven't you heard the rumors?" Char snapped tearfully. Then she softened, struggling to get a grip on herself. "Oh, I'm sorry, Vince. I shouldn't yell at you. None of it's your fault. But the story about me that's going around school — I overheard two girls talking — is just horrible. I can't be seen with any boy, especially you, until I find out who started all this. I have to convince my friends that the rumors just aren't true!"

Vince held his hands up in protest. "Whoa, wait a minute, Charlotte. You're going way too fast for me! I want to help, but first you have to go back and start at the beginning. Just what exactly — "

She shook her head, her blonde curls bouncing vehemently. "I can't talk now. Later. I've got to find Roxanne."

Charlotte whirled around and pushed her way through the heavy curtain before a bewildered Vince could say another word. Just as she hurried down the steps, off the stage, and into the crowd, the already-low lights dimmed even further and the AV crew began rolling the football highlights. Great, Char thought desperately. Now it was going to be even harder to spot Roxanne. But she was determined to find her friend. She had to talk to Rox first, before she braved facing the other girls. Rox would support her. She'd have some sound advice. Why, she'd be as outraged as

Charlotte herself was at the rumor! The reason Roxanne hadn't suspected that anything was the matter that morning when Charlotte raised the subject was probably because no one would dare pass along a story like that to Charlotte's best friend. Rox would have nipped the rumor in the bud if it had come her way.

Charlotte wove her way among the closely packed students, pausing every few steps to stand on her tiptoes and search for Roxanne's auburn head. Some diehard romantics were still dancing, but most of the kids had turned to watch the big screen, cheering as a bigger-than-life Zack completed a pass or ran into the end zone for a touchdown. There were appreciative hoots as the Kennedy cheerleaders, with Stacy front and center, led the fans in a rousing victory chant. Charlotte didn't even glance at the video. Despite all the work she'd put into it and into the whole dance, only one thing mattered to her right now.

And there was Rox! Charlotte's eye was caught by a flash of blue glitter. Sure enough, it was Roxanne's new dress with Rox in it. Char pushed forward eagerly. She started to call Roxanne's name, but then seeing that Rox was head to head in earnest conversation with another girl, she hesitated, not wanting to be rude and interrupt. In the noise and motion of the crowd, Roxanne and the other girl, whom Charlotte now recognized as a former Stevenson student named Marlee Paulson, didn't observe her approach. Charlotte stood quietly for a few seconds. Then she moved to put a hand on Roxanne's arm to get her attention, but stopped dead when she realized that unbelievably, the subject that was absorbing Roxanne and Marlee so completely was *her*, Charlotte. She stepped back to the crowded refreshment table, where she could hear their conversation, but not be seen. If they were talking about her, Charlotte deserved to know what was going on.

"Jana Lacey told me all about what Charlotte DeVries did to you," Marlee was telling Roxanne in a loud, sympathetic whisper. "I know you swore Jana to secrecy, but she said she felt it was her *duty* to let the female population of Kennedy know what Charlotte is really like! I just wanted you to know that I'm terribly sorry. I mean, about what happened with Vince."

Roxanne treated Marlee to a pained sigh. "Thanks, Marlee. I guess I really can't blame Jana for telling people. I only wish someone had warned *me* about Charlotte before I trusted her as my best friend!" Roxanne's wide-set green eyes became curious. "By the way, what exactly *did* Jana say about Charlotte?"

Marlee straightened the gold belt at the waist of her off-white dress, remembering. "Just that Vince isn't the first boy Charlotte's stolen from someone else. Apparently when she lived in Alabama, she broke a couple of hearts a week! I think it's just terrible."

Charlotte saw Roxanne's lips curve in a satisfied smile. "It is, isn't it," Rox conceded, a veiled note of triumph in her low, silky voice.

"I only hope Charlotte gets what's coming to her one of these days!" Marlee declared righteously, patting Roxanne's arm in consolation.

"Oh, she will," Roxanne said with certainty. "She will."

Charlotte stood there, dazed and paralyzed. Could that really be Rox Easton talking? The honest, sensitive person she'd gotten to know at the leadership conference that summer, the girl who'd seemed to need a genuine friend so badly? Was this the kind of friendship Charlotte could expect to receive in return?

The sea of students cheered in unison as the football team's moment of victory was replayed on the screen. Even Rox and Marlee were distracted and pivoted to face the front of the theater.

Charlotte alone walked back the way she had come a few moments earlier, cutting a wide circle around Roxanne and Marlee so they wouldn't see her. This time Charlotte went backstage by way of the tiny orchestra box, not wanting to cross the stage in front of the brightly lit screen in view of the entire Kennedy High School student population.

Vince had waited for her. He was sitting in the folding chair, which now seemed small and rickety next to his large frame. "Did you speak with Roxanne?" he asked, rising to his feet.

Charlotte swallowed, doing her best to maintain her self-control. "Yes . . . I mean, no. I didn't speak with her." She lifted her eyes to stare into Vince's. He had never told Charlotte exactly what had gone wrong between him and Roxanne, why he had broken up with her. For the first time, it occurred to Charlotte that Vince might have learned something about Roxanne, something like she herself had just learned. He would never have said anything that might have harmed Rox's reputation — he was far too kind.

Charlotte knew she could do worse than to follow Vince's gentlemanly lead. She had been ready to spill all her sorrows out to him, and maybe she would tell him the whole story one day. But for now, Charlotte filled Vince in about the rumors without mentioning the role she assumed Roxanne had played in starting, or at least encouraging, them.

By the time Charlotte had finished relating her story, Vince's dark eyes were flashing with indignation. "Wait until I find out who told those lies," he swore, his fists clenched in his pockets. Then he caught sight of the tears sparkling in Charlotte's eyes. "Come here," he said, his voice growing gentle.

A moment later, Charlotte was in Vince's arms. He sat down somewhat precariously on the folding chair, cradling her in his arms. Char felt him kissing her hair and turned her face to his. Their lips met in a deep, sweet kiss. After all the emotional trauma of the evening, Vince's tenderness was almost overwhelming. The tears started again, and Charlotte pulled away from Vince. "You must think I spend about eight hours out of every day crying!" she joked in a weak voice.

"You have a pretty good reason to be upset," Vince assured her. "What we have to do now to make up for it is come up with a few good reasons to be happy." He smiled into her eyes. "How's this for a start?" He kissed her again.

"Pretty good," Char admitted with a half smile. "If the rest of the reasons are that convincing, I'd say we were in great shape!" Then she grew serious again. "I'm afraid a kiss isn't going to erase those rumors, though."

"We'll take care of that together," Vince said purposefully. "I'll help you set people straight. We'll start tonight! There's no time like the present, right?"

"Right," Charlotte agreed. With Vince's arms around her, she felt like anything was possible. Together they could do whatever they set their minds to. Hadn't they cleared out the entire Little Theater by themselves that very day during lunch? They were stronger than any catty rumor. "Let's go!" Charlotte cried.

She wiggled in Vince's arms, ready to rejoin the dance and begin looking for her friends, but Vince restrained her. "Wait a minute," he said. "If you didn't get a chance to talk to Roxanne, what is she going to think when she sees us together?"

Charlotte sighed. Now that a few minutes had passed, the thought of Roxanne made her sad rather than angry. She could imagine what hateful things Roxanne would think, but it didn't matter anymore. "I have a feeling she'll understand," Char said quietly. She stood up and took Vince's hand. From the decibel level at which the music was now blasting, she guessed that the video was over. "Would you like to dance?" Charlotte asked Vince, suddenly shy.

Vince smiled down at her. "I'd love to."

They stepped through the curtain together.

Chapter
14

"Eek!" Lily covered her eyes. She'd seen the old movie version of *Dracula* with Bela Lugosi at least a hundred times, but it still grossed her out every time Dracula bit somebody's neck. This particularly gory bite had taken her by surprise. She'd only been half-paying attention to the movie because she was still thinking over the conversation she'd had with Jonathan earlier that night.

After cautiously removing her hands from her face, Lily leaned forward over her afghan-wrapped legs and grabbed a fistful of popcorn from the large bowl on the coffee table. Then she settled back comfortably against the plump cushions of the den sofa. She and Jonathan had talked for nearly an hour, and by the time they'd hung up, Lily felt confident that she'd convinced him to give the University of Pennsylvania an honest chance. She had pointed out to Jonathan that he couldn't expect to find a replica of the world he'd lived in up until this point. College had entirely new opportunities to offer him, and he'd be missing out in lots of ways if he didn't bother to find out what they were. As for wishing he were still at Kennedy, Lily assured him *that* was simply crazy. Four years of high school was enough for anyone — she herself couldn't wait to move on to the "real world" next autumn!

Jonathan had sounded relatively cheerful when they said good-bye. Lily, though, was emotionally drained. Still, she was glad she'd given up the dance in order to stay home and talk to Jonathan. It had been the right thing to do, whereas meeting Buford would *not* have been the right thing to do, not by a long shot. Talking to Jonathan tonight had made Lily realize all over again how much he needed her, and how much in her own way she still depended on him. So, she had decided to be fair to Jonathan and to herself. She'd keep her promise about not seeing anybody else. At least, Lily thought as she pictured the look on Buford's face the day before when he'd asked her to meet him at the dance, she'd keep her promise until Jonathan came home for Thanksgiving. Then they would have a chance to figure things out face to face.

She munched on the well-salted popcorn, feeling noble and proud of herself for coming to this decision. If there was an element of self-sacrifice involved, she figured she would just have to accept it. But at the same time Lily knew deep inside that while she might hold out until Thanksgiving, after that she wasn't so sure. It wasn't just Buford and the temptation of working with him on *Twelfth Night*, although that was a considerable factor. It was Jonathan himself. As much as she cared for him, she wasn't comfortable in a relationship that restricted her with rules, both those Jonathan forced on her and those she had to force upon herself in order to live up to his expectations. Relationships, Lily had always believed, should free people, not limit them. All these thoughts were pretty hazy in Lily's mind. Jonathan was her first really serious boyfriend; she didn't exactly possess a wide range of romantic experience to fall back on. But her instincts told her that there had to be another way for love to work. Maybe some day she'd discover it.

Dracula got what he deserved, the old stake in the heart, and the movie ended with a blare of melodramatic music. Lily changed the channels aimlessly. She wasn't in the mood for rock videos, or news, or unfunny talk show hosts. Going to bed early with a good book was starting to look like the best option.

Just as Lily switched off the TV with the remote-control, the doorbell rang. Her heart leapt into her throat. It was pretty late for anybody to stop by. Besides, everyone Lily knew was at the Welcome Dance. Not only that, but she was alone in the house. Her parents had gone out to dinner with some out-of-town friends.

Lily approached the front door in what she felt was like super-slow-motion. She clutched the afghan around her shivering shoulders, terrible visions racing through her head. Who was on the other side of the door? She pictured a very tall, unshaven man with a gruesome expression and a large carving knife. It didn't help that she'd just watched *Dracula*.

She put her hand on the doorknob and paused. Maybe she had an overactive imagination, but it was better to be safe than sorry. Instead of opening the door, she shouted through it. "Who's there?" Her voice came out very high and scared-sounding. How embarrassing, Lily thought.

"It's Buford Wodjovodski," came the answer in a reassuringly normal voice. "Is Lily at home?"

Buford! Lily almost collapsed with astonished relief. She hurriedly unbolted the door and swung it open, a giddy smile spreading across her face. "Buford! What are *you* doing here?"

"Hi, Lily!" He grinned back at her through the screen door. "I hope I didn't scare you."

"Oh, no, not at all," she said breezily, her knees still knocking. "But don't tell me you just happened to be in the neighborhood at this hour!"

"No, actually I made a special trip," Buford confessed. "When you didn't show up at the dance, I got a little worried. So I decided to stop by on my way home, since it wasn't too late. I asked two girls I've seen you with at school — I think their names are Stacy and Frankie? — and they told me where you lived." Buford peered at Lily, who was still looking a little pale, besides being bundled up in the afghan like an invalid. "Are you sick?" he asked, concerned.

"No, just a little chilly," she assured him. Just then she realized that, speaking of chilly, Buford was still standing on the front porch, his aviator scarf flapping in the night air. It was a cold evening; the draft from the door was icy on

Lily's bare toes. "Oh, I'm sorry. Do you want to come in for a while?" she invited.

Buford smiled. "I thought you'd never ask. Thanks, I'd love to!"

Ten minutes later, they were both curled up on the sofa with cups of steaming hot chocolate and a fresh batch of popcorn. Lily sipped carefully at her hot chocolate, peeking over the rim of the mug at Buford. Buford Wodjovodski was sitting right next to her on the sofa in her own house! She almost wanted to pinch herself — it just didn't seem possible. She hadn't gone to the dance, so he'd come to her. It had to be fate.

Buford was watching Lily, too. For the first time since she'd known him, she thought he looked just a tiny bit nervous. "So, I really hope it's okay that I came over like this?" he said at last. His tone made the words a question.

"Of course!" Lily responded eagerly. "I didn't make it to the dance because . . . I got a phone call — " She faltered. "Something just . . . came up. But I'm glad you're here now, Buford," she added, meaning it with all her heart. "I really am."

"Good." Buford set his cup down on the coffee table and then leaned toward her, one arm stretched along the back of the sofa just inches from Lily's head. The excitement of his nearness made Lily flush. "Ever since we started working on *Twelfth Night* together, I've been looking for a chance to spend some time with you outside of rehearsals," he continued. He smiled, his bright blue eyes crinkling sheepishly. "Actually, if you really want to know the awful truth, I've wanted to get to know you ever since I saw you in *The Fantasticks* last spring!"

"You're kidding!" Lily exclaimed. She smiled doubtfully. "I don't believe you. I wasn't *that* good!"

"But you were!" he insisted. "Anyway, it wasn't only because you did a great job in the play. There was just something about you. Even though you were onstage, with all that distance between you and the audience, you managed to come across as an incredibly warm, living *person*. I mean, you weren't just another talented actress up there." Buford shook his head. A lock of sun-streaked hair fell across his eyes, and for a brief moment Lily had to restrain an urge to reach up and brush it aside. "I don't know. I guess I really can't explain it."

Buford's praise was more than flattering. It was *personal*. It made Lily feel as if they had known each other somehow, long before they'd ever even met. And not for the first time his words were unintentionally ironic, too: Jonathan had said something similar to Lily about her performance in *The Fantasticks*, when they were first getting to know one another. All of a sudden Lily found herself wondering what would have happened if she had met Buford, as well as Jonathan, last spring. Who would she be seeing now? As much as she adored Jonathan, Lily had a feeling she could guess. It wouldn't have been him.

"Uh, well . . ." Lily leaned toward the coffee table to grab some popcorn, hiding her face and her feelings behind a lock of shiny hair. "Coming from you, a professional actor, that's a nice compliment. Thanks."

"Don't thank me. I'm just saying what's true. Hey, Lily." Buford put a hand on her shoulder. A current of electricity ran through Lily's arm, right down to her fingertips, and she nearly dropped her handful of popcorn.

"Y-yes?" She met his eyes, almost afraid of what might happen next, yet also dying to find out.

"I was wondering. . . ." Their eyes were locked for a long moment. Then his gaze began moving all over her face as if he were memorizing it, and finally came to rest on her eyes again. "I was wondering whether you feel the same way about me that I feel about you."

"What way is that?" Lily spoke softly, almost whispering.

"Like I'd like to know you, be close to you." Buford stopped. He raised a hand and brushed Lily's cheek with one finger. "Know what I mean?"

Lily didn't answer at first. She knew what she should say. She should say that maybe she knew what Buford meant, and maybe she felt the same way, but even so he had to leave her house that minute. She had made a commitment to someone else. Lily had never talked to Buford about her relationship with Jonathan, and it was apparent that he was entirely unaware of her dilemma. Not being part of the crowd, naturally he wouldn't know that she already had a boyfriend. It was up to her to inform him of that fact. *Tell him*, Lily

161

ordered herself. But the words wouldn't come out. Instead, Lily realized she was nodding her head in assent.

Buford didn't wait for any other answer. A moment later, Lily was in his arms and they were kissing. Lily had always heard there were supposed to be fireworks when you kissed someone special, and for the first time in her life she knew what "fireworks" meant. As good as Jonathan had made her feel, he had never made her feel like *this*. Buford's lips were warm and sensitive but firm, and as the kiss deepened, Lily was sure every bone in her body was melting. She was glad Buford was holding her so tightly; she couldn't have sat upright on her own.

They broke apart briefly so that Buford could position a few of the sofa cushions more comfortably behind his back. "There," he said huskily. The smile he gave Lily was both confident and shy, and altogether irresistible. "Now we're all set." He pulled Lily toward him again. The second kiss was even better than the first, and Lily was enjoying it immensely when the telephone rang. She jumped. The blaring ring seemed even louder than usual in the quiet house. She wiggled out of Buford's arms and stumbled in the direction of the kitchen. The lights were out and she had to grope along until her hands hit the phone, mounted on the wall next to the refrigerator. She grabbed the receiver. "Hello?" she said, her voice sounding distinctly panicky.

"Lily, it's me, Jonathan. Did I wake you up?"

Lily's hand started shaking, and she nearly dropped the phone. "No — uh, yes. Sort of. But that's okay." She took a deep breath. She had to sound normal. "What's up? Why are you calling again?"

"I just wanted to say thank you." Jonathan's voice was warm with affection and gratitude. "Thanks for cheering me up. I've been thinking all night about what you said before, about how I wasn't giving college a chance. You were absolutely right and I was absolutely wrong, as much as I hate to admit it!" He chuckled and Lily made herself laugh along with him. Her laughter was hollow, though, and forced. But fortunately Jonathan didn't seem to notice. "I'm ready to start fresh," he continued brightly, "and it's all because of you, Lil."

"I'm — I'm glad, Jonathan," she said weakly.

"Well, that's all! That's why I called. I'll let you go back to bed. You sound kind of out of it."

"I am," Lily had to agree. "But thanks for calling. I . . . I really am glad I could help."

"You did," he repeated with conviction. "I feel much better. You're the greatest."

"Thanks," Lily mumbled. " 'Night, Jonathan."

"Sweet dreams, Lily. I'll talk to you soon."

" 'Bye."

Lily had to fumble around for a few seconds before she located the phone on the wall again and could hang up the receiver. She stood there in the dark — in more ways than one, she thought grimly. Jonathan might be feeling better, but she personally was feeling a lot worse.

She walked back to the den slowly, her bare feet dragging along the cool wood of the hall floor. In the den, the light from the one lamp bathed the room in a low, warm glow. Lily didn't look at Buford as she sat down again beside him on the couch. She didn't want him to read the dismay and confusion that had to be written all over her expressive face.

"Who was that?" Buford asked conversationally.

Lily busied herself with the afghan in an attempt to buy some time. Bringing her knees up to her chin and tucking her feet under the blanket, she bundled herself up cocoon-style. Meanwhile, her mind was spinning. She had so many questions, but no answers. How had she gotten herself into this situation? she wondered hopelessly. How was she going to explain all this to Buford? How was she going to explain all this to *Jonathan*?

"Hello, Lily?" Buford said gently. "Are you still with me?"

Lily turned her face to Buford. She was ready to tell him that it just so happened to have been her boyfriend on the phone a moment ago. It would be an abrupt beginning to the discussion to say the least. Still, she had to start somewhere. But when she met Buford's eyes and he reached for her, Lily realized that there was really nothing to say. Or at least, nothing that couldn't wait until tomorrow. No matter what the circumstances might be, no matter how mixed-up she might feel about the change in her feelings for Jonathan, she wouldn't trade places right now with anyone in the world. She was wild about Buford, and as he touched her she could feel that his emotions were just as strong.

When Buford kissed her again, Lily didn't

resist. She didn't want to. Her anxiety about Jonathan faded somewhat, retreated to the back of her consciousness, and in its place grew a warm, happy glow that was centered somewhere near her heart. Tomorrow was soon enough for explanations, for untangling the strands of her life. Tonight was hers and Buford's — the magical occasion of their first kiss.

As Lily snuggled more closely against Buford's warm, broad chest, she knew that when the time came she'd find the words to say good-bye to Jonathan. It would be painful, and very, very sad, but she could do it. She had to. As for Buford. . . . Where one story ended, another one often began. Lily had the feeling that this moment with Buford was the first page of the most beautiful story she would ever read.

Chapter
15

"So, who's this Beaumont guy?" Daniel asked Lily, raising one dark eyebrow skeptically.

They were lounging on the one comfortable piece of furniture in the newspaper office — a second-hand couch with stuffing projecting from a half dozen holes in the upholstery — after school during the week following the Welcome Dance. Lily had stopped by on her way to *Twelfth Night* rehearsal to talk to Daniel about setting up a picture-taking session with the cast. Sara Gates was to review the play when it opened in a few weeks, but in addition *The Red and the Gold* would include short individual interviews with the students participating in the production. Lily was excited about the publicity, but Daniel wasn't being cooperative about making the arrangements. He'd refused to schedule a date and time for photographing the cast until Lily spilled the beans about the "theatrical-looking dude" she'd been hanging out with recently.

Lily didn't mind Daniel's teasing. They'd been friends, and sometimes enemies, for a long time, having gone to Stevenson together before the transfer to Kennedy. She knew that beneath his sharp-edged exterior, Daniel was as vulnerable as the next person. "Buford, not Beaumont!" she corrected him, giggling. "He's in *Twelfth Night* with me."

"So . . . ?" Daniel sat forward on the sofa expectantly.

"So . . . we're . . ." Lily stuttered to a stop, blushing. "When did you get to be such a busybody, Tackett?"

Daniel grinned. "I'm a journalist. I have a nose for a story!" He gave Lily an appraising once-over. "The evidence is against you, kiddo. I take it that Jonathan is — " Daniel completed the sentence by delicately drawing one hand across his throat, guillotine-fashion.

Lily frowned, her eyes registering her pain. "Something like that," she said quietly.

Daniel dropped his off-hand manner, growing serious. "I'm sorry, Lily. I didn't mean to make light of this deal. Whatever happened. . . . You can tell me when and if you feel like it."

Lily smiled faintly. "Thanks, Danno."

"And, hey, speaking of the latest campus news!" Daniel switched gears. "It looks like Vince finally came through with Charlotte."

"Yeah, isn't that great?" Lily didn't tell Daniel about the intense conversation she'd had with

Charlotte a few days earlier regarding Roxanne's role in spreading the rumor about Char. The girls had straightened it out amongst themselves, and despite Lily's anger — she had never liked Roxanne — she'd agreed with Charlotte, Frankie, and Stacy that the best thing to do was to simply let the issue drop. It was more important to make it up to Charlotte for believing the worst about her than it was to seek revenge against Roxanne. "I think Char and Vince make a perfect couple," she added. "If there is such a thing, that is."

"Yeah, if there is." Daniel sighed somewhat mournfully. Then he resumed his brisk tone. "So, the *Twelfth Night* pictures. Next Tuesday at two-thirty, before your rehearsal?"

"I'm sure that'll be fine, but let me confirm it with Mrs. Weiss and I'll get back to you." Lily bounced out of her seat. "Speaking of which, I'm probably late. I'll see you later!"

"Ciao!" Daniel waved after her. "Have a successful rehearsal. Just remember, 'To be or not to be — that is the question.' "

"Thanks for the tip, Daniel! Wrong play, though!"

"Anytime, Lily."

The door swung shut behind Lily, and Daniel was left alone. The rest of the staff would be wandering in any minute now. The next issue of the paper was due at the printer by the end of the week, and things were starting to heat up again. Daniel was watching himself very carefully this time, however. He wasn't going to make the mistake of taking his frustrations out on innocent bystanders again.

Daniel rolled up the sleeves of his faded black shirt. He had planned to spend the afternoon preparing a draft of the last of the three editorials that would be included in this issue. He reached for a pencil, but when the phone on his desk rang he picked it up instead.

"Is this Daniel Tackett?" a soft, deep female voice asked.

Daniel's heart stopped, and he momentarily lost his breath — as if he'd just been punched in the stomach. Fifty years from now he would still recognize that one-in-a-million voice. It was Lin. He gulped. "Yeah, this is Daniel. Lin . . . ?"

"Yes, it's me. I — it's been a while. How are you?"

Daniel clutched the receiver, his knuckles whitening. "Oh, I'm fine! Just fine. Busy. Another issue of the school newspaper is due next week."

Lin laughed. The low, musical sound sent a shiver of loss and longing down Daniel's spine. "I knew it was a safe bet to call you in the office. I got the number from the front desk," she explained. Then there was a long pause and for a brief, terrible moment Daniel was afraid that Lin had hung up, that he'd lost her again. Desperate, he pressed his face even closer to the phone. When she spoke again, he sank back in his chair, weak with relief. "Um, Daniel I got your letter. I don't really know what to say."

Say anything, Daniel thought, his heart aching. Say anything, just keep talking. I need you — I need to hear your voice. "I'm sorry," he said out loud, his own voice uncharacteristically shaky.

"Was that the wrong thing to do? To write to you, I mean."

"No, not at all," Lin said quickly. "I'm glad you did. It's just that, well, nothing much has changed. I mean, with my parents and all. They don't know you wrote, and they don't know I'm calling you. So I don't know. . . . But I wanted to tell you how much your letter meant to me." She hesitated. A wistful note entered her voice. "I . . . I miss you, Daniel."

"I miss you, too," he said, his heart soaring at Lin's words even as the weight of disappointment settled back on his shoulders. "So much. It seems like forever since the summer and the last time I saw you."

"I know. It does to me, too." Lin stopped, and during the silence that followed, Daniel decided to go for it. He might as well lay all his cards on the table. That's obviously what Vince had done and look where it had landed him. He and Charlotte had finally gotten together.

"Lin, I want to see you," he announced urgently. He was surprised at the depth of his own emotion. "I don't care if your parents don't approve. I mean, I *care*, but I care about you more."

Lin sighed. "Oh, Daniel," was all she said.

Daniel hung his head. He pictured Lin sitting in much the same way on the other end of the phone, her long, silky black hair falling forward over the smooth golden skin of her face. It didn't seem right that there should be so many obstacles between them. "Lin, isn't there any way we could meet? Even for just a little while, just once?"

"Well, I might drive out to Rose Hill for the

Kennedy–Maryville football game," Lin said slowly. "I have a girlfriend who cheers for Maryville. Maybe I'll see you there."

Daniel grabbed at the thread of hope. "Maybe? No maybe about it! You have to come." His voice dropped. "Please come."

"I really think I will." Lin's own tone became more assertive. "It's just a football game, right? My parents can't complain about that!"

"Right!" Daniel practically shouted. "You've gotta show your school spirit."

"Well, then, I'll see you — " Lin stopped speaking abruptly. When she started talking again, she was whispering. "I have to go, Daniel," she apologized. "My mother just pulled in the driveway. She wouldn't understand."

"Until the game, then?" Daniel said hopefully. "Promise me you'll be there."

"Until the game," Lin repeated. " 'Bye."

" 'Bye."

There was a click, and suddenly the line went dead. Daniel continued to hold the phone for a minute. He felt attached to it somehow; it had brought Lin closer to him. Closer, but not close enough. Daniel stifled a dissatisfied sigh. He supposed he should be grateful for small favors. Nothing had been resolved between them. They still might never get together for real. But Lin had broken the ice. Now there was a possibility. Lin had called *him*! Suddenly, deep inside, Daniel started to feel sure that there was more than a possibility. There was hope — genuine hope.

All at once, Daniel didn't feel like spending the afternoon cooped up in the newspaper office.

Maybe he'd actually take a day off from his work. By staying a little bit later over the next few days, he could make up for it. He just had an urge to get outside in the fall air, breathe it, run around in it.

Grabbing his worn leather jacket, Daniel bolted for the door. Halfway there, he put on the brakes. The Kennedy versus Maryville football game — when was it, anyway? It had to be relatively soon.

He backtracked to the big table in the rear of the office where the sports editor sat. The fall sports schedule was taped on the wall; and Daniel scanned it impatiently. Leesburg, Maryville . . . there. He checked the date on the schedule, and then he checked today's date on his watch. The Kennedy–Maryville game was *this* Friday. In only two days, he'd see Lin!

It wasn't like Daniel to make any display of emotion, but there was nobody around to see him, and he just couldn't help himself. "Yahoo!" he hollered, jumping into the air and waving his jacket. "All right!"

He headed for the door again. Before opening it, he smoothed back his shaggy hair and, pulling his Wayfarer sunglasses out of his pocket, positioned them firmly on his nose. On the outside, he was the same cool, impenetrable Daniel Tackett again. But inside, his heart was still pounding with joy. There was hope for him and Lin. All of a sudden, Daniel had a feeling Lily and Buford and Charlotte and Vince might not be the only lucky ones. His senior year at Kennedy could turn out to be the best year of his life.